Francis George Heath

Sylvan Winter

Francis George Heath

Sylvan Winter

ISBN/EAN: 9783337249076

Printed in Europe, USA, Canada, Australia, Japan

Cover: Foto ©Andreas Hilbeck / pixelio.de

More available books at **www.hansebooks.com**

SYLVAN WINTER

WORKS BY FRANCIS GEORGE HEATH.

"Everybody knows Mr. Heath's fascinating books."—Pall Mall Gazette.

FERNS.

                                  s. d.

1. **THE FERN** PORTFOLIO. Imperial Quarto. 3rd Edition 8 0
Illustrated by 15 Plates elaborately drawn life-size, coloured from nature, and accompanied by descriptive text, representing *all the species of British Ferns*, which themselves comprise a large proportion of the ferns of America and of many other parts of the world. ... This work stands alone, for it is the only one ever produced giving *absolute facsimiles* in form, size, colour, and venation of the fronds of ferns.
  "The plates are *wonderful*."—The Author of " **Lorna Doone.**"
  " We need hardly praise 'The Fern Portfolio,' seeing that it is one of the productions of Mr. Heath. ... The volume will be of **great interest** and value."—*Times.*
  " So admirably are the figures drawn and coloured as to **be, for all practical** purposes of comparison, equivalent to the plants which they **copy with such** minute fidelity "—*Knowledge.*

2. WHERE TO FIND FERNS. Illustrated by Fern Plates and **Pictures of** Fern Habitats, &c. With a special chapter on the Ferns round **London** ...   1 6
  " Wonderfully cheap at Eighteenpence."—*Bookseller.*

3. THE FERN PARADISE. Illustrated by Fern Plates **and other En-** gravings, gilt edges. 7th Edition. 12 6
  " All lovers of ferns **will** be delighted."—*Saturday Review.*

4. THE FERN WORLD. **Illustrated by** Fern Plates and other **Engravings,** gilt edges. 7th Edition 12 6
  " Good, well-written **descriptions of our** native ferns."—*Athenæum.*

FLOWERS.

5. SYLVAN SPRING. With Coloured and Wood Illustrations, gilt edges ...   12 6
  " He suffuses his picture with the charm of painting."—*British Quarterly Review.*

FOREST SCENERY.

6. HEATH'S GILPIN'S FOREST SCENERY. Embellished by finely executed Engravings. Cheaper Edition 7 6
  " Mr. Francis George Heath is **an able and accomplished editor.**"—*Standard.*

GARDENS.

7. MY GARDEN WILD, AND WHAT I GREW THERE 5 0
  " A more exquisite picture of the felicity of horticulture has seldom **been** drawn for us. ... filled in with all Mr. Heath's richness of colouring **and** powers of description. ..."—GRANT ALLEN, in *Academy.*

LEAVES.

8. AUTUMNAL LEAVES. Profusely Illustrated by Coloured and **Wood** Illustrations. 3rd Edition 6 0
  " In every way attractive."—*Saturday Review.*
  " Charmingly illustrated. ... Will delight many **eyes.**"—*Spectator.*

PEASANT LIFE.

9. PEASANT LIFE IN THE WEST OF ENGLAND. 5th Edition 6 0
  " A singularly pleasant book to read "—*Queen.*
  " His great art is description."—*Tablet.*

TREES, &c.

10. OUR WOODLAND TREES. Illustrated **by Coloured Plates** and Wood Engravings, gilt edges. 3rd Edition 12 6
  " A work inspired by a genuine and wholesome love of nature."—*Times.*
  " To dip into its pages is like taking a trip to Arcadia."—*World.*

11. BURNHAM BEECHES. Illustrated by Engravings and Map. **Paper** boards, 1s. Holiday cloth Edition, with Author's portrait 1 6
  " Writing with even more than his usual brilliancy, Mr. Heath here gives the public an interesting monograph of the splendid old trees."—*Globe.*
  " The charm of style and perfection of illustration."—*Record.*

12. TREES AND FERNS. Illustrated by beautifully executed **Engravings,** gilt edges. 2nd Edition 3 6
  " A charming little **volume.**"—*Land and Water.*

13. TREE GOSSIP. Typographically ornamented, elegantly bound 3 6
  " **A** series of interesting notes. ... Mr. Heath is a pleasant writer whose capacity to treat upon such topics as are here dealt with has already been proved."—*Times.*

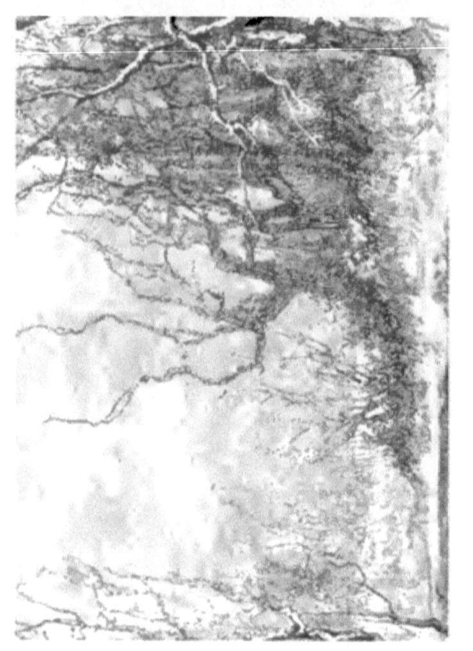

BY

FRANCIS GEORGE HEATH,

EDITOR OF THE NEW EDITION OF GILPIN'S 'FOREST SCENERY;'

AUTHOR OF

'AUTUMNAL LEAVES,' 'SYLVAN SPRING,' 'OUR WOODLAND TREES,' 'THE FERN WORLD,'
'HE FERN PORTFOLIO,' 'THE FERN PARADISE,' 'WHERE TO FIND FERNS,'
'MY GARDEN WILD,' 'TREES AND FERNS,' 'BURNHAM BEECHES,'
'TREE GOSSIP,' 'THE ENGLISH PEASANTRY,'
'PEASANT LIFE,' ETC., ETC.

*WITH SEVENTY ILLUSTRATIONS
BY FREDERICK GOLDEN SHORT,*

ENGRAVED BY JAMES D. COOPER.

London :

KEGAN PAUL TRENCH, & CO., 1, PATERNOSTER SQUARE.

1886.

PREFACE.

AM not surprised that
the ancients worship-
ped trees. Lakes and
mountains, however
glorious for a time, in
time weary—sylvan
scenery never palls.'
So ran, at its conclu-
sion, a remarkable and
interesting letter, which
the late Lord Beaconsfield, in December, 1880,
a few months only before his death, wrote to the
Author of this volume. In the same letter the
distinguished statesman and *littérateur*, turning
from the subject with which he had prefaced
his communication, remarked: 'With regard to
trees, I passed part of my youth in the shade of

Burnham Beeches, and have now the happiness
of living amid my own " green retreats." ' To the
writer's mind, therefore, for the moment, it was
the especial verdancy of spring and summer
which suggested the picture of ' sylvan scenery ;'
and sylvan scenery, to the popular mind, is an
expression which mostly implies the leafiness of
the seasons that precede the fall. Yet the ancient
worship of trees must rather have been suggested
by the stern wintry aspect of the monarchs of
the woods, than by the softer appearance of their
summer clothing—for the strength and power
and grandeur, if the idea may be allowed, of
the tree-form would be more conspicuous when
divested of foliage. Similarly the grandeur and
solemnity of the forest would more powerfully
affect the feelings when the great trunks and
huge limbs of the sylvan giants stood out clearly
defined against the wintry sky. The ' sacred
hunt ' for the venerated Mistletoe was a winter
rite—for that curious parasitic evergreen could not
have been discovered amongst the summer mass
of green leaves ; and the ' sacred fire ' of the
Druids, communicated from the burning Yule-log,

gleamed amidst the sylvan scenery of the cold season.

That Winter is a period of interest and beauty cannot be denied by the student of the woods and fields, though the popular mind regards, perhaps, with little favour the ungenial characteristics of this season.

To point out, however, the especial charm of out-of-door Winter is the aim of the writer of this volume; and in promoting this object, he believes he is calling attention to a neglected subject. In his 'Sylvan Spring' he sought to portray, by pen and pencil, the aspect of the vernal season; in 'Autumnal Leaves,' the especial charm of the season of the fall; and now he hopes he may secure some measure of success in a description of the particular beauty of 'Sylvan Winter.'

THE ILLUSTRATIONS.

ICTURES are so common a feature, in the present day, of every book on every subject, that especial reference to the part they play in the discussion of subjects seems scarcely to be necessary. The illustration should, of course, speak for itself; and whilst it is hoped that those in this volume will not fail in this essential qualification, some explanation of the particular object of their introduction must be given.

In introducing for the first time (in ' Autumnal Leaves ') Mr. Frederick Golden Short's work to the public, the present writer remarked that the Artist, living amidst the most beautiful woodland scenery in this country, had learnt his art from the great book of Nature, and he predicted, from an intimate knowledge of the scenes which Mr. Short had depicted, that those who were equally familiar with these scenes would recognize in this young artist's pictures 'a touch which no mere art-training could give.' The verdict of the press confirmed this estimate, one journal remarking that Mr. Short's graceful sketches were ' instinct with a true feeling for Nature, and full of delicate appreciativeness for quiet English country life.' Of his work for this volume the verdict will not—the Author is convinced, if he may venture to speak for his coadjutor—be less favourable, though the aspect of Nature dealt with is so different. The essential function of art in drawing is not to improve Nature—as some artists, with rare conceit, imagine—but to copy her. Fidelity to the original is, therefore, the best and surest test of artistic ability. To this test the Author begs to submit the work of one who cannot speak for himself.

The initial-letter designs have been made to harmonize with the general purpose of this work, and to exhibit scenery of different kinds, under its wintry aspect, an aspect which, it is desired,

should be natural and not stiff or conventional
—true, that is to say, to life. Here the scenes
selected by the Artist are sometimes wild, and
sometimes instinct with what may be called a
' feeling ' of domesticity. Yet there is no formal
intention to give especial meaning to these little
' bits ' of scenery. They are intended to be typical, in a general way, and that is all.

In the case of the larger drawings, however,
there is a more set and immediate purpose to
subserve, for the accomplishment of which the
Author has sought the particular and painstaking
co-operation of the Artist. This purpose is essentially preceptive, the design being not to introduce pretty scenery, generally representative of
Winter, but to introduce—each in its own familiar
and characteristic landscape—the wintry forms
of prominent and well-known trees. The forms
mostly selected are those of deciduous trees,
because, of course, it is these which exhibit such
marked differences of aspect in summer and in
Winter ; but some evergreen forms—such as the
Cedar, the Stone Pine, and the Scotch Fir—are
also represented, just as types of their class. The

deciduous forms include the Oak, the Ash, the Beech, the Elm, the Birch, the Hornbeam, the Willow, the Poplar, the Chestnut, the Horse Chestnut, the Plane, the Wild Cherry, the Apple, and the Pear, and each has been drawn from the life.

A yet more especial and novel feature of the volume will be found in the twig drawings. From the general wintry form of the tree, as shown in the landscape drawings, we descend to the parts, in order to give, in more minute detail, the salient characteristics of the ramification. The drawings of twigs comprise the Oak, Beech, Elm, Ash, Birch, Lime, Chestnut, Sycamore, Willow, Alder, Blackthorn, Hawthorn, Hazel, Maple, Hornbeam, Larch, Horse Chestnut, Plane, Poplar, Mountain Ash, Apple, Cedar, Yew, and Scotch Fir. These, it will probably be admitted, are sufficiently wide and representative, and, in conjunction with the other special drawings and studies, will, it is hoped, not merely please, but instruct the reader and the student.

It may be accepted as sufficient evidence of the quality of the engravings to mention that the work has been done by Mr. Cooper.

LIST OF ILLUSTRATIONS.

INITIAL-LETTER DRAWINGS.

TWIG DRAWINGS.

FULL PAGE LANDSCAPE DRAWINGS.

SMALLER LANDSCAPES.

CONTENTS.

PART I.

SYLVAN WINTER.

PART II.

WINTER WOOD LORE.

PART I.

SYLVAN WINTER.

SYLVAN WINTER.

I.

WINTRY OUTLOOKS.

INTER, as it is presented to the mind in its ideal form, is commonly associated with thoughts of cold and frost; of cutting wind and chilling rain; of snow - covered fields and ice-bound streams and lakes; of barrenness, bleakness, and cheerlessness. When Shakespeare refers to 'The Winter of our discontent'

B 2

an idea of the dead season is conveyed in a manner which suggests the simpler notion of *desolation* in its abstract form. Barnard admirably conveys the general idea in the lines :—

> ' The dead leaves strew the forest-walk,
>   And wither'd are the pale wild flowers ;
> The frost hangs blackening on the stalk,
>   The dew-drops fall in frozen showers ;
> Gone are the spring's green sprouting bowers,
>   Gone, summer's rich and mantling vines ;
> And autumn, with her yellow hours,
>   On hill and plain no longer shines.'

To those who view Nature from a distant outlook, and regard her with cold and unsympathetic eyes, Winter is doubtless presented under an aspect like that of a desert, or of a barren moorland held under the chill grip of all-pervading cold—a region given up to lifelessness and gloom.

Thomson, in his ' Winter,' expresses the same idea when he says :—

> ' Dread Winter spreads his latest glooms,
> And reigns tremendous o'er the conquer'd year.
> How dread the vegetable kingdom lies :
> How dumb the tuneful : Horror wide extends
> His desolate domain.'

Yet in the same poem he conveys the idea of Winter as presented to the intellectual mind :—

> ' All Nature feels the renovating force,
> Of Winter, only to the thoughtless eye
> In ruin seen.   The frost-contracted globe
> Draws in abundant vegetable soul,
> And gathers vigour for the coming year.
> A stronger glow sits on the lively cheek
> Of ruddy fire; and luculent along
> The purer rivers flow : their sullen deeps,
> Transparent, open to the shepherd's gaze
> And murmur hoarser at the fixing frost.'

But even here it is the physical benefits conferred by Winter, and not its scenic beauty, that stress is laid upon : and our poets have mostly waxed eloquent upon the ' dread ' and ' chill ' aspect of the dead season.   Cowper paints a terrible picture, yet fringes it with silver in the last two of the following lines :—

> ' Oh, Winter ! ruler of the inverted year,
> Thy scatter'd hair with sleet-like ashes fill'd,
> Thy breath congeal'd upon thy lips, thy cheeks
> Fringed with a beard made white with other snows
> Than those of age ; thy forehead wrapp'd in clouds,
> A leafless branch thy sceptre, and thy throne
> A sliding car indebted to no wheels,

> But urged by storms along its slippery way ;
> I love thee, all unlovely as thou seem'st,
> ·And dreaded as thou art.'

' All unlovely as thou seem'st ' again pictures the popular idea, though ' I love thee ' implies the discernment of beauty unsuspected by the careless passer-by. Yet the expression ' A leafless branch thy sceptre ' implies a severity of opinion intended to strip the subject of any idea of interest or beauty. To the ' leafless branch,' however, we shall look, in the succeeding pages, for a large store of the symmetry and beauty which go to furnish the external aspect of Sylvan Winter.

George Crabbe gives expression to the ideas so largely prevalent amongst our poets when he says :—

> · When Winter stern his gloomy front uprears,
> A sable void the barren earth appears ;
> The meads no more their former verdure boast,
> Fast bound their streams and all their beauty lost.'

Here truth is clearly subordinated to poetical effect. Rhymsters are far too frequently the slaves of their rhymes. The same writer paints almost as black a picture as that drawn by Thomson in the lines already quoted from his 'Winter.' It is in his 'Inebriety' that Crabbe's lines occur, in which he gives the following terrible view, and the verse succeeds the one just given :—

> 'From snow-topp'd hills the whirlwinds keenly blow,
> Howl through the woods and pierce the vale below,
> Through the sharp air a flaky torrent flies,
> Mocks the slow sight and hides the gloomy skies.'

Ably descriptive as are all these verses of the harsher aspects of Winter, they seem to the present writer to err only in so far as they give a general character to particular features ; but this error is widely made by poets who conceive that Winter is all black and dismal, that it has no brighter side, and that if there be brighter intervals they are 'unseasonable.' The popular though erroneous notion of a forest is that of land covered uninterruptedly with trees. Forest, in fact, is country of a mixed kind, and may include woods, heaths, moors, mountains, and streams. So Winter is a season of a mixed character, and may include different kinds of

weather, mostly cold but not always or necessarily
so, and by no means given up to the uninter-
rupted reign of frost and snow. It would be
contrary to the purposes of Nature were all the
world held under the icy grip of cold during
the whole of the wintry season. The genial
intervals which unthinking people are in the
habit of calling 'unseasonable,' are a quite
necessary part of the wise economy of things,
during what to the vegetable and to the bird and
insect world is mostly a season of rest. Nature
could no more endure the constant presence of
severe cold during what are called the winter
months than it could the steadfast prevalence of
scorching sun in the summer. How often has
the clouding of the sky and the cooling of the
wind in the last-mentioned season been welcomed
as a wise and necessary relief from the solar
glare! and how often, on the beneficent principle under which the coldness of the wind is
tempered to the shorn lamb, is the coldness of
what is called but is only partly—in truth—the
' dead season,' tempered to meet the varying requirements of animated creation! Yet the sea-

son is not changed by the changes of temperature and aspect. Now and then there is what seems a violent change in character. Frost and snow will sometimes reign uninterruptedly for many weeks with exceptional severity, and at other times the character of the weather, during nearly the whole of the season, is more autumnal than winterly. But it may be said that it is not the particular season but the cycle of seasons which makes up Winter in its proper acceptation.

Wintry outlooks, therefore, in the view we here adopt, do not mean only scenes of frost and snow and of bleakness and barrenness, of misty air and leaden skies. They mean also blue skies and sunny air; scenes of beauty in the graceful leafless forms—spreading over the landscapes—of deciduous trees; and the brightness and sparkle of the evergreen loveliness which boon Nature displays in many a nook and angle to maintain perpetual verdure for the comfort and happiness of mankind.

II

LEAFLESS WOODS.

LEAFY forest, Gilpin remarks, in his 'Forest Scenery,' * is not solely the object of incidental beauty. 'The picturesque eye,' he quaintly adds, 'finds great amusement even in its wintry scenes, when it has thrown its rich mantle aside, and appears, to the common eye, naked and deformed.' This last expression —'naked and deformed'—happily conveys the popular idea of the forest in Winter. Bare

* 'Heath's Gilpin's Forest Scenery,' page 348. The subsequent references to 'Forest Scenery' are also to the present writer's edition.

ground strewn with dead leaves, and the naked forms of trees, are all that the unobservant pedestrian sees in his walks through wintry woods. Except in search of sport, and, then, gun in hand, he does not attempt to walk through when the ground is covered with snow, and frost holds the air. When the air is crisp and the ground is dry he will often do so, but in search of exercise and not of beauty. Yet the careful study of winter woodlands is delightful. Gilpin, in continuing the remarks just quoted, provides some pleasant suggestions for the early riser on a winter day. 'The hazy sunshine of a frosty morning,' he says, 'is accompanied by an indistinctness peculiar to itself. The common haziness of a summer day spreads over the landscape one general grey tint; and, as we have had occasion to remark in different circumstances, is often the source of great beauty. But the effect we are here observing is of a different kind. It is generally more partial—more rich—and, mixing with streaks of different coloured clouds, which often form behind it, produces a very pleasing effect. The case is, the sun is lower in the horizon and produces an effect which a meridian sun cannot do.' But it is not merely the general effect of the play of sunshine—through clouds— upon the forest as a whole that is noticeable ; for the peculiarities of individual trees add largely to the beauty of the scene. Gilpin does not say very much upon the wintry aspect of the forest, but what he does say is well worth quoting. 'Great beauty also,' he remarks, 'arises in Winter, from the different tints of the spray. The dark-brown spray of the Birch for instance has a good effect, among that of a lighter tinge ; and, when the forest is deep, all this little bushiness of ramification has, in some degree, the effect of foliage.' He adds, 'The boles of trees likewise, and all their larger limbs, add, at this season, a rich variety and contrast to the forest ; the smooth and the rough, the light and the dark, often beautifully opposing each other. In Winter the *stem* predominates, as the *leaf* in summer. It is amusing in one season to see the branches losing and discovering themselves among the foliage ; and it is amusing also, in the other, to walk through the desolate forest, and see the various combinations of *stems*—the traversing of branches across each other in so many beautiful directions—and the pains which Nature takes in forming a *wood* as well as a *single tree*. She leaves no part unclosed; but pushing in the branch or the spray as the opening allows, she fills all vacant space and brings the heads of trees, which grow near each other, into contact; while every step we take presents us with some beautiful variety in her mode of forming the fretted roof under which we walk.'

Very beautiful, in its suggestiveness, is this language of the delightful writer on 'Forest Scenery.' 'The pains which Nature takes in forming a *wood* as well as a *single tree*'—the italics are Gilpin's. Those who notice such things at all must often have remarked when planting any little spot in a garden or park how quickly Nature—kind Nature in this as in everything—undoes the clumsy work of the planter. Be he ever so deft in arranging the positions of the plants he wishes to grow and the relations of these to each other, he cannot—it is *impossible*—however artistic and tasteful may be his method, put them just as Nature would have them, and as he—the planter—admits when, sometimes after a few days, sometimes after a few weeks, and sometimes it may be after months and years, he looks at them arranged as Nature wills. Whether the place planted be a little rockery of small herbaceous plants, a garden bed, a whole garden, or a park or wood, the eye at once detects the hand of the planter. Branches and leaves appear to be all awry. But Nature quickly steps in and with exquisite grace and symmetry arranges the whole. 'She leaves no part unclosed.' Here is the secret. The expression 'Nature abhors a vacuum' has often been used. Her office is to leave nothing unutilized; and in the woods she is constantly seeking, as elsewhere, to fill every space; yet in such a way as to cause no confusion and little jostling. The season of growth is, of course, the period when these symmetrical and beautiful arrangements are made. The vigorous shoot that is to form the limb, the ramifications of those that are to form the branches and twigs, all co-operate to make up the perfect whole.

Spring and summer, as we have said, manufacture; but it is Winter that discloses the work, in the deciduous forest. Then, and then only, can we see the entire effect, because the garment of leaves has been thrust aside and Nature holds her exhibition—free to all—of form ; and its finest effect is seen in the forest which has been untouched by the hand of the pruning forester.

It is this close and intimate view—which the free exhibition of Nature discloses to the interested and delighted student—that opens up the marvellous variety conspicuous, not only in the forest as á whole, but in individual trees even of the same kind. Gilpin says, in his description of what he calls the 'picturesque beauty' of trees, that 'though every animal is distinguished from its fellow by some little variation of colour, character, or shape, yet in all the *larger parts*, in the body and limbs, the resemblance is generally exact. In trees it is just the reverse; the *smaller parts*— the spray, the leaves, the blossom, and the seed— are the same in all trees of the same kind, while the larger parts are wholly different. You seldom

see two Oaks with an equal number of limbs, the
same kind of head, and twisted in the same form :
and it is from these larger parts that the *most
beautiful varieties* result.' *

Conspicuous, of course, amongst the leafless
denizens of the forest is the Oak, and its ruggedness and grandeur impress, alike, all who look
upon it with interest.   It appears to and does hold
the ground as no other tree does.   Its power is
amazing—its enormous tap-root penetrating the
ground and holding it in place so firmly as to
enable it to defy the tempest.   From its great
bole—fashioned with such peculiar strength and so
admirably adapted to meet the force of hurricanes
—spread, in their enormous amplitude, the limbs ;
from these the twisted branches, and from the
branches the contorted spray.   Of the especial
stoutness of the ' King of the Forest' Gilpin has
something characteristic to say.   In speaking of
this he remarks: ' A second characteristic of
the Oak, of which Virgil takes notice, is the
stoutness of its limbs; its *fortes ramos.*   We
know no tree, except perhaps the Cedar of

* ' Forest Scenery,' page 4.

ОАБ.

Lebanon, so remarkable in this respect. The limbs of most trees *spring* from the trunk. In the Oak they may be rather said to *divide* from it; for they generally carry with them a great share of the substance of the stem. You often scarcely know which is stem and which is branch; and towards the top, the stem is entirely lost in the branches. This gives particular propriety to the epithet *fortes* in characterizing the branches of the Oak; and hence its sinewy elbows are of such peculiar use in ship-building. Whoever, therefore, does not mark the *fortes ramos* of the Oak, might as well, in painting a Hercules, omit his muscles. But I speak only of the hardy veterans of the forest. In the effeminate nurslings of the grove we have not this appearance. There, the tree is all stem, drawn up into height. When we characterize a tree, we consider it in its natural state, insulated, and without any lateral pressure. In a forest trees naturally grow in that manner. The seniors depress all the juniors that attempt to rise near them. But in a *planted* grove all grow up together; and none can exert any power over another.'

Such special mention the Oak demands in our dealing with the general wintry aspect of the forest because it is a dominating figure. We entirely agree with Gilpin that it is 'the most picturesque tree in itself, and the most accommodating in composition.' He rightly adds that 'it refuses no subject either in natural or in artificial landscape. It is suited to the grandest, and may, with propriety, be introduced into the most pastoral. It adds new dignity to the ruined tower and Gothic arch; by stretching its wild, moss-grown branches athwart their ivied walls it gives them a kind of majesty coeval with itself. At the same time its propriety is still preserved if it throw its arms over the purling brook or the mantling pool, where it beholds

'"Its reverend image in the expanse below."'

In the leafless woods the grandeur and robustness of the Oak, so greatly exceeding that of other trees, serves to establish contrasts which are all the more striking because the 'King of the Forest' forms a foil, or background, so to speak, that establishes a basis of comparison with the gracefulness and symmetry of the Beech, the lightness and elegance of the Ash, the delicate beauty of the Birch, and the contorted picturesqueness of the Hawthorn. Of these all, in turn, and of many others, we shall speak in the succeeding chapter. Here we take note only of the forest as a whole, or of the wood or copse which forms part of the forest. The individual tree can be studied by itself in that detail which the interest of the subject demands ; but to get a good and comprehensive view of the whole so as to fully appreciate the exceeding beauty of the forms unclothed by the mantling foliage of summer, not only in themselves, but in their relations to others, it is through leafless woods that the inquirer must direct his steps.

III.

EPHYRS that gently touch the summer leaves of the forest give the charm of movement to the varying shades of verdure which spread over the landscape and impress the brain, through the eye, with that sense of beauty which lends such fascination to summer foliage. But the still air of a frosty day, when the atmosphere is freed from fog or mist, provides the best condition for studying the beautiful forms of trees.

First, by right of magnificence must come the tree that reigns in the forest—the noble Oak.

The saplings of most trees foreshadow the characters which become pronounced as age creeps on. The stem of the young Oak is often twisted; its bark is grey in colour, and somewhat rough. Its buds are irregularly placed along the branches, the spray being rather abundant but stout, and the buds not large but prominent; the smaller branches growing from each other at obtuse angles and, twisting picturesquely, showing thus early, though remotely, the ruggedness of the mature tree. These characters are continued and maintained during the middle age of the Oak, and emphasized as it approaches old age and decay. Mr. Short's drawing of the Oak, in the landscape engraving facing page 16, happily conveys the picture of the tree in its prime. The powerful yet rugged trunk, the stalwart limbs, the irregular forking—now acute, now rectangular—of its branches, the twisting yet robustness of the spray, are all excellently shown. In the picture, facing page 32, of ' a dead Oak stump,' the artist has, with equal truthfulness, seized the still salient features, strong, so to speak, in death. How well this drawing exhibits the grim tenacity of this sylvan giant, which

though dead is still firmly rooted to the earth,
showing no weakness or decadence in its aspect,
but seeming to throw up its limbs with defiant
uprightness! Gilpin asks : 'What is more beautiful on a rugged foreground than an old tree with
a *hollow trunk?* or with a *dead arm,* a *drooping
bough,* or a *dying branch?*' In Mr. Short's study
from life of a dead Oak stump, the foreground is
not rugged but soft and beautiful, for it is running
water. It is the tree which is rugged, and which
at once centres upon itself the admiration of the
onlooker.

From the Oak it is natural to come to the
Beech, and, facing page 48, in the engraving representing Beeches in 'a flooded stream—evening,'
the most prominent figure in the foreground may
be termed a character study. Rugged sometimes,
especially in the contortions of its roots—characters strongly represented in the famous Burnham
Beeches—the Beech is most remarkable for the
gracefulness and symmetry of its form. The
divisions of the trunk towards the ground, somewhat like the fingers of a hand, are very peculiar,
but the furrows soon disappear as the trunk goes

upwards, and enables the clear, smooth stem to rise with the beautiful symmetry by which it is distinguished. It is the smooth, greyish-white skin of the Beech which has tempted visitors to the woods to engrave their names upon the bark. One prominent and striking character of the tree, besides the smoothness and beauty of its bole and limbs, is its frequent habit of forming a trunk of double columns. Oftentimes, quite close to the ground, the bole divides and carries far up aloft with graceful vigour and uprightness the two trunks, both of which, spreading outwards, form, by their ample ramifications, a head of considerable width. The Beech has always had a reputation for beauty; it is a tree, as Gilpin happily described it, 'of picturesque fame.' Yet, strange to say, the author of 'Forest Scenery,' with an eye so quick to discern beauty, disliked the Beech, and made it the subject of some very severe criticism. He says : 'In point of picturesque beauty I am not inclined to rank the Beech much higher than in point of utility. Its trunk, we allow, is often highly picturesque. It is studded with bold knobs and projections, and has, sometimes, a sort of

irregular fluting about it, which is very characteristic. It has another peculiarity also which is
sometimes pleasing—that of a number of stems
arising from the root. The bark, too, often wears
a pleasant hue. It is naturally of a dingy olive;
but it is always overspread, in patches, with a
variety of mosses and lichens, which are commonly
of a lighter tint in the upper parts and of a deep
velvet-green towards the root. Its smoothness,
also, contrasts agreeably with these rougher appendages. No bark tempts the lover so much
to make it the depository of his mistress's name.
It conveys a happy emblem—

  ' " Crescent illæ ; crescentis amores." '

'But, having praised the trunk, we can praise
no other part of the skeleton. The branches
are fantastically wreathed and disproportioned,
twining awkwardly among each other, and running often into long, unvaried lines, without any
of that strength and firmness which we admire
in the Oak, or of that easy simplicity which
pleases in the Ash; in short we rarely see a
Beech well ramified.' *　Gilpin remarks, however,

  * ' Forest Scenery,' pages 65-6.

that 'contrary to the general nature of trees, the Beech is most pleasing in its juvenile state, as it has not yet acquired that heaviness which is its most faulty distinction. A light, airy young Beech with its spiry branches, hanging, as I have just described them, in easy forms, is often beautiful. I have also seen the forest Beech, in a dry, hungry soil, preserve the lightness of youth in the maturity of age.'

In the editorial remarks in 'Forest Scenery,' the present writer has expressed the opinion that for some reason Gilpin entertained a prejudice against the Beech. In some points that author's criticism is incorrect, and his deductions from his admissions are not, in the present writer's opinion, consistent. The 'dingy olive' hue, is not the natural hue of the Beech bark, but is imparted to it, more or less, by the lichens which stain it, so to speak. The 'fantastical' wreathing of the branches, too, adds, we think, to its 'picturesque beauty,' and few who have seen a fine and characteristic Beech wood in Winter would be inclined, we believe, to deny that the scene was one of singular beauty. The grooved and pillared columns—moulded, in their softness of contour, like human limbs—rising amidst the wreathed contortions of their roots, from the brown, leaf-strewn floor of the forest, now singly, and now in double and treble lines, and forking into branches, which, bending and curving and twisting, fling out against the sky a fretwork roof of myriads of boughs and spray, present a sight not easily forgotten by those who have seen these delightful trees in all their native freedom, untouched by the hand of the pruning woodman.

'The Venus of the Woods,' as the Ash has been called, next claims, we think, some notice. 'Ashen-grey' is an expression sufficiently familiar to denote the peculiar tint of the bark, which is more clear and conspicuous in young, than in old trees. The smoothness of the young ashen bark is also another feature, and a mark, too, as in the case of the skin of the Beech, of beauty. But the Ash sapling has less beauty in its form than the mature tree, because of the thickness and scarcity of the spray, and the prominence of the buds, which are larger in proportion than those of the full-grown Ash ; but it nevertheless has a sleek and graceful look. It is not the young tree, however, but the older tree of the woods (page 64) that has claimed the admiration of lovers of Nature, and earned the distinctive and complimentary appellation of this beautiful species. Though it is in its summer dress, with its delicate-looking pinnate leaves, that it has been most admired, the gracefulness which is its especial character when clothed in its summer verdure is sufficiently apparent in what may be termed its wintry undress. The height of the tree is often, and indeed generally, a prominent characteristic. Frequently the bole rises to a considerable distance from the ground before forking. It may then give forth branches so large as to appear like the first fork of the trunk, so nearly do they approach the trunk's diameter. Rising still higher, before what may be called the actual forking takes place, the bole may divide into two nearly equal limbs, and it is only there that the continuity of the trunk is fairly broken. Each limb will then divide again, and the forking will be continued and repeated from limb and branch, and twig and spray. The continuity of the subdivision occasions considerable length, and as with length there is necessarily weight, there is a consequent drooping, which gives a very graceful character to the tree. Yet the central and upper branches stand erect with considerable vigour, and the spray, in consequence of the length and slenderness of the shoots, is curved oftentimes by the effort to keep an upright position after drooping. Probably it is the combination of acute angles and curves that helps to give to the Ash its easy and graceful aspect. It is in the lower part of the tree that the branching makes the most acute angles. As the limbs and branches become lengthened, however, they spread outward and commence to droop, and it is this character which, observable throughout all the ramification, gives its peculiar gracefulness to the ' Venus of the Woods.'

If the boy be father to the man, the sapling may also be said to be the parent of the tree, and, with few exceptions, to exhibit those peculiarities, though softened by youth, that make the maturer growth characteristic. As with other trees, so with the Elm. The young tree exhibits the uprightness of growth, and the peculiar angular ramification, together with the shortness of the spray, so especially characteristic of the full-grown Elm. Very beautiful is the form of the mature tree, (page 80), as seen growing naturally with all its limbs, and without the lopped or maimed appearance too frequently noticeable in our hedge-row Elms. The main stem is sometimes divided near the bole, and sometimes nearly half-way towards the top, but the division is irregular. When the division takes place higher up, the superior length of bole gives to the tree a degree of dignity, which, combined with the rugged bark and the bold angles made .by the limbs and branches, serves to make it a striking object. If the bole be short, enormous limbs parting from it stand out from the trunk at, sometimes, a broad angle and with an expansive spread upwards and outwards, almost suggestive of the Oak, with the ruggedness and pictu-resqueness of which old Elms frequently vie—the branches, twigs, and spray twining and twisting in a zigzag fashion, very much after the manner

of the Oak, whilst the bark not only on the bole
limbs and larger branches, but upon the smaller
ones, is split and cracked and flaked in a way
that gives it an eminently picturesque appearance.
We must add to our own remarks Gilpin's
opinion of the tree. He says that ' the Elm
naturally grows upright, and when it meets with
a soil it loves, rises higher than the generality of
trees ; and after it has assumed the dignity and
hoary roughness of age, few of its forest brethren
(though, properly speaking, it is not a forester)
excel it in grandeur and beauty.'

The beauty and gracefulness of the Birch,
(page 64), are very striking, and in the whole
forest there is probably no tree whose delicacy
of form is equal to that of *Betula alba*. The
purple spray and the curious whiteness (accompanied sometimes by splashes of golden lichen
and spots of brown) of the bole are at once the
most striking peculiarity of this tree, though bole
the Birch can scarcely be said to have ; for the
entire stem, from base to apex, is so evenly
graded as to leave no line where the bole may be
said to end, and the upper part of the stem to begin.

Strictly speaking, perhaps, the whole of the stem of a tree is its bole. Yet ordinarily the thick, stout, and lowermost part of the stem is commonly understood when the expression 'bole' is used. Sometimes, the stem of the Birch is very upright, but, as often, it is somewhat bent out of the perpendicular, and thus acquires what Gilpin calls a more 'picturesque' aspect. The branches, symmetrically disposed around it, are long, light in form, slender, and as finely and regularly graded as the trunk itself. From the branches the spray, upon the same principle, is symmetrically and elegantly graded, but in spite of the length and fine gradation of the ultimate branchlets, they share, with the whole, a certain irregularity or waviness which pleases the eye. It is the delicate lightness of the branches and spray, and their susceptibility to the slightest motion of the wind, that give to the Birch its especial grace and beauty when seen in its wintry form.

A very graceful tree is the Lime. Its rich, dark-brown bark hardly loses its peculiar and elegant smoothness until the tree has reached a considerable age. All trees, as their age increases, become more subject to accidents, which affect the proportion and symmetry of their forms. A certain brittleness in the wood of the Lime renders this tree peculiarly subject to injury, and hence certain disfigurements are not unfrequently noticeable in large and full-grown specimens; but when it has emerged from the sapling stage to that of the tree, and before it has acquired a stem of more than three feet or so in girth, it is an object of great beauty. Its branches, symmetrically placed around its trunk, are thrown out with a graceful sweep (rising, bending, falling) from all sides. From the branches the abundant spray proceeds in the same symmetrical manner, giving an elegant aspect to the whole tree. In larger trees the bark is more rugged, and sometimes a double stem, rising from a junction with the bole commencing within two or three feet from the ground, gives a variation from the normal form of the single trunk. In larger and older trees there is observable a ruggedness both of trunk and of ramification; and twists and bends and angles are observable both in the large limbs and

A DEAD OAK STUMP.

in the smaller branches. The ramification itself is considerable and abundant. Equally, from all sides of the trunk, proceed the main limbs ; from these a second set of stout branches, making broad angles with the former; then the twigs, standing out at similar angles; and finally the bud-pointed spray, divided off on the same plan, —the whole combining to give an aspect of subdivision that is most complex and beautiful.

Like many trees in the case of large specimens, the base of the Lime bole is channelled, and appears, so to speak, to claw the earth. The absence of low side-branches, owing to the accidents already referred to, arising from the brittleness of the wood, detract, as this tree gains age, from its appearance; and often, for a considerable distance up, this tree's branches are scanty and irregular, if not absent altogether. But compensation in such cases is afforded by the head, where the branches, too small oftentimes to be called limbs, are thrown out with much grace, not in curves or flowing lines, yet not ruggedly, but with a certain picturesque irregularity—the wealth of twigs and spray, gracefully displayed, giving a striking and beautiful aspect to the tree-head.

But when large trees, as is sometimes the case, have grown up free from accidents causing deformities, they present forms of great beauty. We have seen trees forking at eight feet from the ground, and forking again eight feet further up into solid limbs three feet in diameter at their base. These, spreading away from the main stems, arch gradually upwards and outwards, the forking continuing on the same plan by gradation to the ultimate spray, until a head of great breadth and beauty is produced. Gilpin's opinion of the Lime is that it is 'an elegant tree where it is suffered to grow at large; but,' he adds, 'we generally see it in straight bondage, clipped into shape, and forming the sides of avenues and vistas.'

However, he thinks that 'in its best state it is not very interesting. It has a uniformity of surface, without any of those breaks and hollows which the most picturesque trees present, and which give their foliage so much beauty.' The author of 'Forest Scenery' is here alluding to the summer aspect of the tree ; but though we do not agree with his judgment, even of the foliaged Lime, and believe that the trees he had seen had probably been clipped at some time without his knowledge, it will be easily understood that, whilst the fullness of the ramification would give a greater density to the Lime when in leaf, the beauty of the wintry form would be perfectly transparent and all the greater for the abundance of the spray.

In its young and in its full-grown state, the Hornbeam (page 96) has a rugged, horny, and singularly picturesque aspect. Possibly the toughness of its wood has given rise to its common name, which, popularly rendered, would be ' horny tree ;' but another reason for its designation might be found in its peculiar ramification, which is very suggestive of the branching of horns. In appearance as well as in reality, it is hard and tough.

The trunk of the Hornbeam is mostly striated, the bark being raised in ridges which look like swollen veins. The limbs are stout in proportion to the bole, and are twisted and wide-spreading, first upwards, and then outwards and downwards. On the extreme branches the twigs sometimes almost touch the ground, whilst the spray, like the branches, is long, fine, picturesquely twisted, much divided, and very abundant,—the whole forming a spreading, sweeping, and very graceful head—every little space being filled up with bough or twig, and uniformity of gradation being everywhere preserved and maintained between trunk, limbs, branches, and spray. On the Hornbeam, as on some other trees, occur occasionally the dense clusters of small twigs on the larger branches, looking, at a distance, like birds' nests.

Another 'picturesque' tree, when seen in its mature form, is the Common or Field Maple, which, Gilpin rightly says, is 'an uncommon tree, though a common bush.' Most familiar in hedge-rows as a common bush, it is not often seen of tree-size. Even when a sapling its branches have a straggling and somewhat rugged appearance, characteristic of its mature form. Gilpin quaintly adds to the sentence quoted above, 'We seldom see it employed in any nobler service than in filling up its part in a hedge, in company with thorns and briars and other ditch trumpery.' Yet the ancients, he admits, held it in great repute, Pliny speaking as highly of the knobs and excrescences of this tree, called the *brusca* and *mollusca*, as Dr. Plot (in his 'Natural History of Oxfordshire') did of those of the Ash. Of the size and character of the Maple, Gilpin expresses himself as follows: 'In the few instances I have met with of this tree in a state of maturity its form has appeared picturesque. It is not unlike the Oak, but is more bushy, and its branches are closer and more compact. One of the largest Maples I have seen stands in the church-yard of Boldre in New Forest; but I have not met with specimens enough of this tree to form an opinion of its general character.' The Maple in Boldre Churchyard is still living, and is larger than in Gilpin's time. A drawing of it by Mrs. Lister Kay appears in the view of the church and churchyard of Boldre published in the present writer's edition of 'Forest Scenery.' Under-neath this famous tree lie the mortal remains of Gilpin and of his wife.

The ramification of a finely-grown Field Maple (page 112) is very complex, and the whole tree is exceedingly picturesque. The rough-barked trunk, widened at its base, where it holds the ground, rises, gradually tapering, by a series of twists like the meandering of a river through rocky country. It commences to branch ordinarily at some six feet from the ground, and the branches (sometimes large enough to be called limbs) take different directions. If of large size, and partaking of the character and substance of the trunk, the limbs will take an upward direction; if branches only, they will often shoot out, like those of the Oak, almost at right angles from the stem; but whether the direction be parallel or horizontal, the branches are always of considerable length by comparison with the trunk, and proceed with twists and forks and contortions. From the larger branches, smaller ones, equally twisted and bent, are given off; and from these, twigs of varying length, which in turn break into small short spray half an inch to two or three inches in length—the spray, like the rest of the ramification, being bent, twisted, and contorted. Thus the whole of the spreading head of the Maple is filled with a most beautiful, elaborate, and complex network. The tree is not high, but often spreads considerably, and in this, as in its zigzag, contorted aspect, very much resembles the Oak.

Its near relative, the Sycamore, ought to be mentioned next to the Maple. A well-grown specimen is round and handsome in form, clawing the ground by the peculiar channelling of the trunk which is common to many trees. The bark is tolerably smooth and often rendered green by the presence upon it of lichen-growths. Oftentimes the trunk rises to a considerable height before it loses its continuity and commences to divide into limbs. In instances where the forking commences at a half or at one-third of the total height of the tree, the branches which form the division are disposed so regularly around the stem, and are so moderate in thickness, that they give a handsome and symmetrical appearance to the tree. The direction upwards of the branches of the Sycamore exhibits that slight irregularity which especially occasions what is termed picturesqueness. There is no twisting or contortion, but just the slight irregularity which gives interest and variety to natural forms. The limbs are thrown outwards and upwards at a somewhat acute angle from the trunk, and extend oftentimes to a considerable distance from it, sweeping and spreading in a manner that adds dignity to the tree, though sometimes the branches and boughs are so slender in proportion to their length that they immediately begin to droop—thus giving gracefulness and beauty of another kind. The limbs are disposed irregularly around the trunk, and the branches around the limbs in the same manner, and the angles and directions of each to, and in relation to, each aid that variety which pleases the eye. There is not much subdivision of the ramification of the Sycamore, the general character of the twigs and spray being robust, and the contrast not so great as to give the peculiar beauty incident to abundant spray. Gilpin's opinion of ' the Great Maple, commonly called the *Sycamore*,' is that it 'is a grander and nobler tree than the Smaller Maple,' just mentioned ; but he thinks that ' it wants the elegance ' of the Field Maple, and is ' coarse in proportion to its bulk.' He adds, that 'its bark has not the furrowed roughness of the Oak, but it has a species of roughness very picturesque.'

A sort of deciduous Cedar the Larch (page 240) might be termed, if regard were had, in its relationship to other trees, to its leaves. It is, of course, a not distant relative of the Cedar, because, like it, it is a conifer. The ramification of the Larch is very peculiar and picturesque—the branches spreading so regularly around the straight, upright bole as to present a strongly-marked conical appearance. In comparison with the trunk the branches are thin—there are no limbs properly so called—and they are long and sweeping. On leaving the stem they rise slightly for the space of an inch or two, and then dip, the lowest part of this dip being at a considerable proportional distance from the stem. Rising again, the branches take a long sweep upwards and outwards. The gradation in thickness of both stem and branches is very gradual. Each branch is divided on very much the same principle, but as the twigs grow horizontally with relation to the branch, a flat appearance is given to the latter.

From the branches the spray depends gracefully, and produces an appearance which may be likened to water streaming over a rock. Perhaps the expression 'spray' may have had its origin in some fancied resemblance of the smaller ramification of a tree to the showers of water at a waterfall. Attached to each twig on the Larch, like beads strung sparsely upon string, are the small protuberances which indicate the position of the buds; whilst hung here and there in the meshes of the spray are the pretty cones, sometimes dependent, and sometimes erect, or nearly so. It is the droop in a species of festoons of the Larch spray that gives the flat appearance to the upper side of each branch; for though the smaller branches grow all around the larger ones, their length and weight make them droop, especially as they are also weighted by the twigs that grow out from them. It is, of course, the slenderness in proportion to the length of the branches and twigs which causes the droop. The entire aspect of this tree is graceful, beautiful, and striking. To our own account of this elegant tree we must add an extract from Gilpin's description. He says :* 'I shall conclude my account of deciduous trees with the Larch, which is a kind of connecting species between them and the race of evergreens. Though it sheds its leaf with the former, it bears a cone, is resinous, and ramifies like the latter.' (He means like the conifers.) 'It claims the Alps and Apennines for its native country, where it thrives in higher regions of the air than any tree of its consequence is known to do—hanging over rocks and precipices which have never been visited by human feet. Often it is felled by the Alpine peasant, and thrown athwart some yawning chasm, where it affords a tremendous passage from cliff to cliff, while the cataract, roaring many fathoms below, is seen only in surges of rising vapour.' Permeated with his sometimes quaint, occasionally peculiar, but always charming notions of the 'picturesque,' Gilpin considers that the Larch is only 'fully picturesque when the storms of many a century have shattered its equal sides and given contrast and variety to its boughs.'

* 'Forest Scenery,' page 97.

But if we would consider next a really 'picturesque' tree, and one that has not obtained, so far as we know, any reputation for winter beauty, we should select the Plane (page 128), the leafless aspect of which is singularly and exceptionally beautiful and striking, on account mainly of the zigzag character of its ramification. The bole is oftentimes very long, and it tapers gradually with a series of gentle turns. From irregular points all round it, the branches are given off. They may be called limbs, but they are not large ones. As they ascend, they become twisted, proceed in curves, and then, continuing, droop alternately in rounded and also in angular form ; rise again, dip once more, and finally rise and droop and rise again. The branches give off zigzag boughs, which proceed in the same manner, turning, twisting, bending, and rounding. Twigs and spray follow a similar course, and the final result is that the whole space occupied by the outline (enclosed, that is to say, within the outlines) of the tree is well filled by its ramification, which, though irregular and picturesque, is nevertheless symmetrical; for there is systematic gradation from bole to limbs, from these to their branches, and from branches to twigs and spray. The peculiar and well-known peeling from the trunk, and from the larger limbs, of the bark further adds to the striking and interesting aspect of this tree. The author of 'Forest Scenery,' speaking of the two species of Plane with which he was familiar—the Occidental and Oriental Planes, describes them as 'noble trees;' of the first named he says: 'Its stem is very picturesque. It is smooth and of a light ash colour, and has the property of throwing off its bark in scales, thus naturally cleansing itself— at least, its larger boughs—from moss and other parasitical incumbrances. This would be no recommendation of it in a picturesque light, if the removal of these incumbrances did not substitute as great a beauty in their room. These scales are very irregular, falling off sometimes in one part and sometimes in another; and as the underbark immediately after its excoriation is of a lighter hue than the upper, it offers to the pencil those smart touches which have so much effect in painting. These flakes, however, would be

more beautiful if they fell off more in semicircular
laminæ. They would correspond and unite
better with the semicircular form of the bole.'
Gilpin further says : ' Its lower branches,
shooting horizontally, soon take a direction to
the ground ; and the spray seems more sedulous
than that of any tree we have by twisting about
in various forms to fill up every little vacuity
with shade.' This refers to its summer procli-
vity. We do not agree with the author of
' Forest Scenery ' in our opinion of the result
as shown in Winter, for he says : ' At the
same time it must be owned the twisting of its
branches is a disadvantage to this tree, as we
have observed it is to the Beech, when it is
stripped of its leaves and reduced to a skeleton.
It has not,' he continues, ' the natural appearance which the spray of the Oak and that of
many other trees discovers in Winter ; though I
have heard that in America, where it grows
naturally, it grows more freely and does not
exhibite that twisting in its branches.' It is
strange that Gilpin should here object to that
twisting of the branches of the Plane that in other

cases he considers to be an element in a picturesque effect; but this feature cannot possibly be other than a ' natural appearance.'

The Poplars are an interesting group, well worthy of some attention. Amongst the family no individual is more deserving of notice than the Lombardy Poplar (pages 52, 128, and 144). Its tall, straight, and pointed stem, and its accompaniment of branches closely attached to, and abundantly produced all around it, give it a conical figure, which is strikingly and conspicuously prominent. Oftentimes the branches commence to grow almost from the very base of the stem, and it is their clustering habit and their habit of growing at so sharp an angle from the trunk of the tree that gives the Lombardy Poplar so remarkable an appearance. The clothing of branches is continued from the base to the very apex of the stem, but they never attain to a size which warrants their being called limbs; and as it is seldom the habit of the tree to fork, and each branch is invested, on the same principle as the stem is clothed, with smaller branches, all of which make sharp angles with the trunk, the denseness and

peculiarity of the ramification are very striking.
'Its conic form,' Gilpin says, 'is peculiar.'
'Among evergreens,' he adds, 'we find the
same character in the Cypress, and both trees in
many situations have a good effect. The Cypress
often, among the ruins of ancient Rome, breaks
the regularity of a wall or a pediment by its conic
form; and the Poplar on the banks of the Po, no
doubt has the same effect among its deciduous
brethren, by forming the apex of a clump; though
I have been told that, in its age, it loses its
shape in some degree and spreads more into a
head.' Of course in Winter the figure of this
handsome tree is less prominent, and makes a less
noticeable figure as seen outlined against the sky,
than when clothed in its heavy garb of leaves;
but the wintry aspect, though more light and
elegant, is not less interesting and remarkable.

Very nearly related to the Lombardy Poplar,
the Black Italian Poplar (page 144) is noticeable
from it by its wide-spreading branches. Similar
in many of its characters to the tree just described,
it differs in the essential one, that its branches
grow more sparsely, are stouter in proportion to

BEECHES. (A FLOODED STREAM—EVENING.)

the stem, and start from the latter at much broader angles ; but when finely grown and unbroken by the wind or by the lopping woodman, its ramification is beautiful and symmetrical. Frequently the stem is tapered from the base to the apex with striking regularity and uniformity, and scarcely makes the slighest curve from a vertical position. The branching commences very low down on the trunk; but in the case of a tree of any size, such, for instance, as one with a bole three feet in girth, all branches within six feet of the ground will have dropped away. The branches of the Black Italian Poplar are produced equally around the stem, and though sometimes slightly waved, are often equally straight; but they curve upwards at their points with a graceful sweep. The angle of distance from the trunk is about forty-five degrees. A distinctly conical shape (though a much broader cone is formed than is the case with the Lombardy Poplar) is produced by the incidence of the branches, the lowermost being longest and the length being lessened gradually towards the apex of the stem. The twigs start from the branches at the same angle as that of the latter from the stem, and the spray is given off at a similar angle from the twigs, and all—branches, twigs, and spray growing from all sides of stem, branches, and twigs with uniform regularity—produces a roundness of form which gives an especial aspect of symmetry and grace to this tree.

A handsome and striking object, when seen as a full-grown tree, is the Abele Poplar (page 160). Its trunk, oftentimes rising to a considerable height, almost erect, or bent but slightly from the perpendicular, occasionally reaches a height of fifty feet before commencing to branch. Taking a long sweep upwards and outwards, the limbs fork irregularly in opposite directions, divide into stout branches and these into long, pendant spray. The limbs, after forking, stretch away from each other at wide angles, branches parting from these on the same principle, and the length of the resulting twigs and spray causing the drooping of the latter. The spray from the lower branches often droops considerably, giving a weeping character to this part of the tree, not always shown to quite the same extent in the upper branches.

The parting of limbs, branches, and spray is almost rectangular in many parts of the tree, and this, combined with the length of the branches, and the weight of their complement of twigs and spray, is the cause of the drooping which is a noticeable feature of large specimens of the Abele Poplar. When the tree is old and the bole large, the bark, as in the case of most old trees, is deeply grooved and wrinkled, and the abundant presence of green lichen in the moist grooves gives a rich colour to the trunk. The bark of the young spray is naturally an olive-green.

Of the Willows, whose name is legion, only one, whose fame has gone far and wide, can be mentioned—the beautiful Weeping Willow. Even of Weeping Willows the varieties are innumerable, but all we shall attempt to do will be to indicate a few characters especially applicable to these trees in general. Ordinarily the bole is not long and oftentimes it is massive, and at a short distance from the ground it parts at wide angles into two or more large limbs, which take many twists and picturesque turns that give a rugged appearance to the tree. The limbs

divide into long branches, these into long boughs,
and the latter into long, fine spray.　The smaller

Lombardy Poplars.　Willow.

boughs and the spray droop
in graceful festoons, and it is
perhaps the contrast afforded by the twisting and
somewhat contorted character of the larger limbs

and the fine depending branches and spray, that gives so peculiarly graceful a character to the latter. The bark of the trunk and limbs is seamed and scarred in fine old specimens, and is green with the incrustation of lichen, whilst the bark of the boughs and spray is smooth, shining, and olive-green in colour. It is the wide angles at which the ramification is produced that gives its spreading habit to the tree. Very much the same in general character, with the exception of the pendulous habit, is the ordinary Willow; but in its case, when it grows close to the water's edge, as in the specimen drawn in the engraving on page 52, there is more or less of drooping in its habit, especially when, as is frequently the case, the trunk leans over the stream or lake by which it is situated. Then there is a general inclination towards the water of trunk, limbs, boughs, and spray. This position is doubtless often caused by the softening of the earthy habitat on the side next the water, through the washing of the stream or the motion of it by the agency of wind—if the water be a lake. Less support to the trunk being furnished on that particular side, the weight of the tree, and not unfrequently the force of the wind, carries it gradually, as its age and weight increase, towards the water and gives to it the pendulous habit it would not otherwise have.

'The Weeping Willow,' the author of 'Forest Scenery' thinks, 'is a very picturesque tree,' but he does not consider it (he was doubtless referring to it in its summer dress) 'adapted to sublime subjects.' He, however, considers that ' the Weeping Willow is the only one of its tribe that is beautiful.'

Very handsome, but with a peculiar and decided character in its ramification, is the Wild Cherry Tree (page 112). The lower part of the bole is channelled and appears, as is the case with trees already mentioned and others, to hold the ground as if by claws. Its stem rises erect and tapers gradually, giving off equally all around it, with perfect regularity, branches which are first arched and then droop. The tree would thus assume a weeping form, but for the turning up, more or less, at the ends of the boughs, of the twigs and spray. The angles made by the branches with the trunk are very broad, nearly, in most cases, and in some cases quite, rectangular. Being abundant and parting from the branches on the same principle, the twigs and spray form a complete canopy of interlacement, and when the tree is looked up into from underneath, a very elegant appearance is produced, which has a beautiful effect. The bark on the trunk, even of large Cherry Trees, is smooth, except in places where it has peeled off, though by a curious arrangement the splitting of the bark takes place not longitudinally but horizontally, and looks at a distance like a number of rings investing the trunk. The roots near the trunk often, for a distance of several feet, rise above the ground, and thus serve to increase the especial picturesqueness of this tree. Sometimes the trunk, as in the specimen facing page 112, parts in two at a very acute angle, and each fork rises so erect—each giving off branches from time to time—from the point of division as not, in the smallest degree, to detract from the very symmetrical appearance of the tree.

Ruggedness and picturesqueness are the characteristics of a well-grown Acacia. The bole, spreading out at the bottom into rugged claws, rises straight, though gnarled and twisted, showing upon its surface many hard-looking knobs and protuberances, whilst the bark is rough, grooved, and contorted (page 176). Sometimes at about ten feet from the ground the stem forks into limbs, which again branch—the branches dividing into smaller ones and these into spray on the same plan—one of twisting angularity and contortion, rising, twining, bending, drooping, and rising again. Yet though rugged, all is symmetrical—there is no irregularity or inconsistency, and all spaces are well filled by twisted limb, branch, or spray. The spread of the tree is not great, yet it is enough to give an ample character to the head, and its height —including trunk and superimposed branches—is not meagre. From the sides of the trunk, beneath the first principal fork, branches are not unfrequently given off, and these rise, bend, droop and twist in the same picturesque manner as is noticeable in the entire ramification. So curious is the twisting of the bark on the bole and limbs, that the ridges stand out like a network of ropes wound upon the trunk. Here and there the

brittleness of the wood, a recognized characteristic of this tree, is shown by snapped-off
branches—not the larger, as a rule, but the smaller
ones; but the absence of these scarcely detracts
from the symmetry of the Acacia as seen at a
distance. The torn and rugged appearance of
the bark may be likened to what the trunk would
look like had it been dragged over huge, sharp
rocks. Its dark-brown colour is set off by the
green lichen which spreads in patches over it.
In the case of this tree, as in that of the Lime,
some of the apparent angularity of the ramification is not real; for branches snapped off at
their junction with a limb give an idea of contortion
when in reality there is none; but, nevertheless,
twisting and sudden bending are real characteristics of the tree. Sometimes in the process
of twisting, the branches double on themselves
and double back again, thus approaching occasionally a form that may be likened to that of
the letter S.

The appellation of 'a noble tree,' which Gilpin
gave to the Chestnut when 'in maturity and perfection,' is not too high praise; and that its wintry

form is not less grand in its degree than its form
in the season of leafage will, we think, be admitted by the reader who glances at the faithful
figure given in the drawing, which our artist has
made, facing page 192. The rugged trunk clawing
the ground, the twisted, contorted, and stalwart
limbs, the rugged and drooping boughs and spray
—all twining, arching, twisting, and bending—are
happily shown in Mr. Short's sketch. Gilpin's
remark that it grows like the Oak is not inappropriate, though the Chestnut falls short of the Oak
in the immense proportions and in the strong
rectangular growth of the limbs. He says, 'Its
ramification is more straggling, but it is easy.'
This is very true, as our drawing will show, for
the form delineated has not the stern grandeur of
the Oak.

Of the Horse Chestnut in its wintry form
(page 59) the author of 'Forest Scenery' does
not speak, but under its rich garb of Summer
leaves he calls it 'a heavy, disagreeable tree,' an
opinion from which we have elsewhere dissented.*
Stripped of its leaves it presents one particular

* 'Forest Scenery,' page 88.

feature which is peculiar and noticeable. Its lower limbs, which start from the part where the bole ends, and, in a somewhat less prominent degree, its upper ones, first rise, then arch, and

Horse Chestnut.

then droop and rise again. It is doubtless the rapidity of its growth and its remarkable vigour that give to young trees of this species their

striking robustness and uprightness. There is
then no spray, for all the shoots are stout, and
the ramification is simple and not abundant. At
the base of each branch and twig the skin is
curiously wrinkled, like the cast skin of a silk-
worm, and immediately under each branch and
offshoot is the strange-looking mark so strikingly
like the figure of a horse-shoe, namely, a half-
disc with a row around its curved edge of spots
like the nails placed in the shoe of a horse. It is
doubtless this very peculiar appearance which has
obtained for this tree the otherwise inappropriate
name of the Horse Chestnut.

The contorted, picturesque Hawthorn, with its
twisted trunk and its twisted, spreading head,
must not be forgotten in our examination of
wintry trees that denude themselves of foliage to
exhibit the beauty of their form. As a bush or
shrub the Hawthorn is very familiar to everybody,
but usually in a form clipped out of its natural
and normal shape to meet the exigencies of a field
or garden fence. In the forest alone does it grow
in full freedom and assume its tree-form, and then
it may boast a bole nine feet in circumference,

though specimens have been found with a circumference of twelve feet. Gilpin, so quick to discern
picturesque beauty, was strangely oblivious of
that of the Hawthorn. He says: 'The Hawthorn should not entirely be passed over amidst
the minuter plants of the forest, though it has
little claim to picturesque beauty,' and he considers, oddly enough, that 'its shape is bad.'
Possibly he may only have been familiar with the
disfigured shrub (whose shape is bad indeed), so
unmercifully clipped out of all naturalness; but
if he never saw the full-grown, perfect tree, he
should, at least, in the surroundings of his forest
home, have seen such gnarled and twisted and
pre-eminently picturesque forms of Hawthorn as
that shown, with Ivy, facing page 208. We
must defend a beautiful and striking shrub even
against the candid opinion of the genial author
of 'Forest Scenery.'

Let us now briefly speak, in the enumeration
of the forms of tree beauty, of the familiar
Pear and the not less familiar Apple (page 62).
The curious arching of the branches of the Pear,
as they rise from the rugged trunk, bend, dip,

Pear.   Apple orchard
(misty moonlight).

and rise again,
must often have
been observed
by those who note such things,
and the strangely picturesque
form of the Apple, too—with
its straggling, twisted trunk, and its wide-spreading,

contorted arms, covered, all, by the splashes of
golden and silver-grey lichen, is equally familiar.
Beautiful as, in each case, these useful trees are
when covered by spring blossom, summer leaf,
or mellow autumn fruit, they are interesting and
beautiful, too, when all the especial charm of the
sunny seasons has left them, and they stand in
the simple, unclothed guise of wintry form.

IV

EVERGREEN BEAUTY.

EW, Cedar, Pine, Fir, Holly, Ivy, and Box may, perhaps, be called the most typical and prominent of the Evergreens, which add so much brightness to what is nevertheless called the 'dead season.' These do not by any means stand alone as the verdant ornaments of Winter, but they have the first claim to notice.

The Yew, quite unjustly, has fallen under the displeasure of the poets. Blair, in his 'Grave,' says,—

'Cheerless, unsocial plant! that loves to dwell
'Midst skulls and coffins, epitaphs and worms;

ASH.
BIRCH.

> Where light-heel'd ghosts and visionary shades,
> Beneath the wan, cold moon (as fame reports)
> Embodied thick, perform their mystic rounds.
> No other merriment, dull tree! is thine.'

There is, however, a gleam of admiration in some lines of Wordsworth :—

> ' Of vast circumference and gloom profound,
> This solitary tree !   A living thing
> Produced too slowly ever to decay ;
> Of form and aspect too magnificent
> To be destroyed.'

The popular idea seems to associate the Yew with death and the graveyard, and 'no other merriment, dull tree, is thine,' in the lines just quoted, appears to imply that only ''midst skulls and coffins, epitaphs and worms,' is this tree to be found, just as the carrion crow is associated with death and putrefaction. But it is forgotten that it is the hand of man which has placed the Yew in the midst of its surroundings of mournfulness and gloom, and that it is naturally a forest tree.   In its praise we could write a very long chapter, but we can only give to it its proportionate space in this brief history of the evergreen beauty of sylvan Winter. Very beautiful indeed we consider the dark-green, glossy foliage of the Yew. The leaves themselves are quite as beautiful as those of the much-praised Silver Fir, and, like them, are flat, but are pointed instead of round at their apices. They are produced in double rows along the twigs, are slightly stalked, dark-green above (except when newly produced), lighter underneath, and curved upwards from the back of the twigs. How brightly they shine when the earth is bound by frost and snow, gleaming forth from the chillest surroundings with a delightful freshness, suggestive of their enduring life and vigour: how patiently they bear overshadowing of foliage above, that would kill many other plants, looking vigorous and green and beautiful under the most depressing circumstances: and how persistently they adorn the branches of the noble tree which bears them—pervading emblems of verdancy—must be fully known by those who would fairly appreciate the sylvan beauties of the Yew.

Dear old Gilpin comes warmly to the rescue of this tree from aspersion. ‘As to its picturesque perfections, I profess myself (contrary, I suppose, to general opinion) a great admirer of its form and foliage. The Yew is, of all other trees, the most tonsile. Hence all the indignities it suffers. We everywhere see it cut and metamorphosed into such a variety of deformities, that we are hardly brought to conceive it has a natural shape, or the power, which other trees have, of hanging with ease. Yet it has this power in a great degree, and in a state of nature, except in exposed situations, is perhaps one of the most beautiful evergreens we have.' Writing about the Yew, the author of 'Forest Scenery' puts in a sensible plea for the colour of this tree's foliage. He says, 'But though we should be able to establish its beauty with respect to form and foliage, there remains one point still which we should find it hard to combat. Its colour, unfortunately, gives offence. Its dingy, funereal hue, people say, makes it only fit for a churchyard. This objection, I hope, I have already answered in defending the colour of the Scotch Fir.* An attachment to colour, as such, seems to me an indication of

* 'Forest Scenery,' page 116.

false taste. Hence arise the numerous absurdities of gaudy decoration. In the same manner a dislike to any particular colour shows a squeamishness which should as little be encouraged. Indeed, when you have only one colour to deal with, as in painting the wainscot of your room, the eye, properly enough, gives a preference to some soft, pleasant tint, in opposition to a glaring, bold one; but when colours act in concert (as is the case in all scenery), red, blue, yellow, light green, or dingy green, are all alike, the virtue of each consists solely in its agreement with its neighbours.' *

One little extract from the charming writings of Mr. Leo Grindon must be given in support of the theme of praise which has been here attempted of the beautiful Yew. In his 'Trees of Old England' Mr. Grindon says, 'Nature gives the Yew a very different abiding-place from the cemetery; and rightly viewed and understood, perhaps, the Yew may prove, after all, notwithstanding its possession of deadly sap, to be a tree that should contribute ideas rather of cheerfulness than of

* 'Forest Scenery,' pages 128-9.

mourning. Upon rugged limestone scars and cliffs, where nothing else, save a little Ivy, can establish anchorage, the Yew is often seen clinging, as if bound to the rocks with clamps of iron. Well-nigh flattened against the perpendicular face of the stone, and with the merest ledge or crevice for its feet, it holds itself unchanged for centuries, and is the most imposing picture nature affords of imperturbable endurance. So, too, upon many a remote hillside, beaten and ravaged by tempests, exposure to the wrath of the elements seems congenial, and life in the midst of perils to be joy and strength.'

No tree, perhaps, adds so much grandeur to the sylvan aspect of Winter as the Cedar of Lebanon (page 70), though there are many that add as much beauty. It is a tree that at once arrests the attention, and perhaps the peculiar sombreness of its foliage, and the striking manner in which it is arranged, are the particular features which interest and attract. The broad spread and droop of the branches, the expansiveness of the top, and the remarkable arrangement in layers (which catch and absorb the light) of the branches, give to the Cedar an aspect which, once seen, is not easily forgotten. When, as is some-

Cedar of Lebanon.

times the case, this noble tree is seen standing alone on the face of some stretch of greensward, the bright green of the grass, shining through the spaces be- tween the branches, brings out in strongly contrasting colours the sombreness of the evergreen Cedar foliage. The massive

character of the solid trunk is another feature
of importance. Sometimes the trunk rises erect
to a height, it may be, of nearly twenty feet
before branching, and then it divides into enormous limbs, partaking of the character of trunks
in their massiveness and solidity. From the
points of division of these, two or three other
enormous limbs may rise erect, whilst others,
leading off all round at nearly right angles, again
divide into large branches, and these into stout
offsets, the whole stretching far away from the
trunk and preserving the spreading and noble
habit of the tree. Looking up under a large
Cedar, one is impressed by the sight of the
interlacing network of limbs and branches, and
of the shadowy spread of the leafage above and
beyond.

Nearly related to the Cedar of Lebanon and to
the other beautiful species of the genus *Cedrus*
(the Indian and the Mount Atlas Cedars), the
Pines afford, by the evergreen character of their
needle-shaped leaves, bright and delightful examples of the perennial verdancy of Nature. Their
number and variety preclude anything like a

detailed description of them in these pages, but two must be mentioned as in some sort representatives of the others. Let us take the Scotch Fir or Pine, as it really is, as typical of many others in so far as its general characters are concerned. There is a peculiar beauty and symmetry in this tree in its early form. The somewhat rough, reddish-brown bark already foreshadows the richness of colour of the mature tree. The branches are produced in whorls, usually of five in each whorl, upon the upright stem. Upon these grow the needle-shaped leaves, each pair of leaves sheathed at their bases. The leaves are produced all round the branches which bear them, and are from two to three inches long, narrow, bluish-green, striated. By this method of arrangement on the branches the latter have a cylindrical appearance, so regularly are the leaves disposed. From the base to the apex the stem is gradually and elegantly tapered, and this circumstance, taken in conjunction with the regular and systematic arrangement of the branches, gives a strikingly symmetrical appearance to the young tree. Later in its life it loses this symmetrical beauty. From the full-grown trees (page 224) the side branches mostly fall, leaving a trunk still more or less erect, and marked by its reddish hue, and with spreading heads formed by twisted branches and irregularity of boughs and leaves. Mr. Short has admirably portrayed the Scotch Pine as it is mostly seen in the forest. His drawing is a picture, the central beauty of which consists of the figures of two specimens of *Pinus sylvestris.* One glance will suffice to show that these trees are eminently calculated to please, as Gilpin expresses it, 'the picturesque eye.' Of the Scotch Fir he says, 'For myself, I admire its foliage, both the colour of the leaf and its mode of growth. Its ramification, too, is irregular and beautiful, and not unlike that of the Stone Pine, which it resembles also in the easy sweep of its stem, and likewise in the colour of the bark, which is commonly, as it attains age, of a rich reddish-brown. The Scotch Fir, indeed, in its stripling state, is less an object of beauty. Its pointed and spiry shoots, during the first years of its growth, are formal; and yet I have sometimes seen a good contrast produced

between its spiry points and the round-headed
Oaks and Elms in its neighbourhood. When I
speak, however, of the Scotch Fir as a beautiful
individual, I conceive it when it has outgrown all
the more unpleasant circumstances of its youth,
when it has completed its full age, and when, like
Ezekiel's Cedar, it has formed its *head among the
thick branches.* I may be singular in my attachment to the Scotch Fir; I know it has many
enemies, and that may perhaps induce me to be
more compassionate to it; however, I wish my
opinion in its favour may weigh no more than the
reasons I give to support it.'

Umbrageousness is the distinguishing character
of the Stone Pine (page 240). Indeed, the name
of Umbrella Pine is particularly well earned, for
not only the expansive and sheltering spread
of its sombre-green foliage, but the direction
taken by its limbs resemble strongly the head-
covering and framework of an umbrella. The
trunk is short and stout, and the limbs are given
off from it at very wide angles, and, from the
point of intersection with the top of the bole,
proceed at once in curves outwards and upwards.

The lowest limbs are the longest, as they have further to go to reach the level of the others, for the head of this Pine is nearly flat, and the branching and arrangements are very similar to the umbellate form of inflorescence. The whole form of the tree is more or less round, and the limbs are divided on the same plan as the trunk, and the branches on the same plan as the limbs. The bark is seamed and very rugged, and the whole aspect of the tree is handsome. The elegant appearance of the long, fleshy, needle-shaped leaves, inserted, in twos, in short, brown sheaths, adds to the beauty of the Stone Pine. Another peculiarity is that the leaves are produced not all along the sides of the twigs, but in tufts at the end of the spray. The trunk, after giving off large and even ponderous limbs, sometimes continues to rise in a more or less erect manner, dividing finally into limbs, branches, twigs, and spray, in the same manner as before. Gilpin has much to say of the Stone Pine. He takes it into consideration next the Cedar of Lebanon. 'The Stone Pine,' he remarks, 'promises little in its infancy in point of picturesque beauty. It does not, like most of the Fir species, give an early indication of its future form. In its youth it is dwarfish and round-headed, with a stout stem, and has rather the shape of a full-grown bush than of an increasing tree. As it grows older, it does not soon deposit its formal shape. But as it attains maturity, its picturesque form increases fast. Its lengthening stem assumes commonly an easy sweep. It seldom, indeed, deviates much from a straight line, but that gentle deviation is very graceful, though, above all other lines, difficult to trace. If accidentally either the stem or any of the larger branches take a larger sweep than usual, that sweep seldom fails to be graceful. It is also among the beauties of the Stone Pine that, as the lateral branches decay, they generally leave stumps which, standing out in various parts of the stem, break the continuity of its lines.'

Of its foliage Gilpin says, it ' is as beautiful as the stem. Its colour is a deep, warm green, and its form, instead of breaking into acute angles, like many of the Pine race, is moulded into a flowing line by an assemblage of small masses.

As age comes on, its round, clump head becomes more flat, spreading itself into a canopy, which is a form equally becoming. And yet I doubt whether any resinous tree ever attains that picturesque beauty in age which we admire so much in the Oak. The Oak continues long vigorous in his branches, though his trunk decays; but the resinous tree, I believe, decays more equally through all its parts; and in age, oftener presents the idea of vegetable decrepitude than of the stout remains of a vigorous constitution. And yet in many circumstances, even in this state it may be an object of picturesque notice. Thus we see in the form of the Stone Pine, what beauty may result from a tree with a round head and without lateral branches, which require indeed a good example to prove. When we look at an Ash or an Elm, from which the lateral branches have been stripped, as is the practice in some countries, we are apt to think that no tree with a head placed on a long stem can be beautiful; yet in Nature's hands (which can mould so many forms of beauty) it may easily be effected. Nature herself, however, does not always follow the rules

of picturesque beauty in the production of this
kind of object. The Cabbage Tree, I suppose, is
as ugly as the Stone Pine is picturesque.'

Of the many other beautiful species of Pine,
mention must be briefly made of one or two.
And first 'the Remarkable Pine'—*Pinus in-
signis*—claims notice, whose foliage is produced
in beautiful tufts of leaves of four and five inches
long, the tufts produced symmetrically at the ends
of the whorled branches, and looking like elegant
tassels. The Austrian Pine—*Pinus austriaca*—is
another species, with long, deep-green leaves
which, produced all round the stems, give a
handsome and bushy appearance to its branches,
whilst for the beauty of its long and drooping
foliage, nothing excels the splendid *Pinus excelsa*,
whose name speaks for its qualities.

Amongst the Firs which are distinct and beautiful in their characteristics, the Silver Fir and
two of its varieties demand first mention. The
dark-green glossy leaves of the normal species,
with their white-lined undersides—streaks of
'silver'—the leaves disposed in double rows
along the sides of the twigs that bear them;

Picea nordmanniana with pyramidal form, whorled branches, and leaves upon them, ornamentally twisted, and produced all round the stems, but showing by their twisting habit the white, silvery streaks of the undersides against the rich, bright golden-green of the upper sides, and against the reddish-brown colour of the branches, the normal green of the foliage being occasionally tipped with a golden hue—beautiful, crowded, and much-divided branches sweeping outward and curving downwards: *Picea nobilis*, equally beautiful, and not unlike the one just referred to, but with a tint of darkish green; and the Spruce Fir—*Abies excelsa* —whose remarkably symmetrical form, upright stem, and round branches, thickly covered by its verdant foliage, the leaves evenly disposed all round the irregularly whorled branches, fine-pointed and needle-shaped—these are some of the more prominent species of the beautiful Firs.

There are none who need be told how much the beauty of Winter is enhanced by the charming Holly, whose brilliancy lights up the darkest corners of the woods; by the deep green of the perennial Ivy, and by the delightful foliage, where

seen in its wild state, of the Box.   Things of beauty,
too, are the opening leaves of Primroses, which in
sheltered corners of the woodland, even when the
thermometer is at zero, are oftentimes fresh and
delightful.   Looked at casually, primrose-leaves in
mid-Winter are refreshingly suggestive of light
verdancy; but examined more closely, we can discern the beautiful and appropriate fashioning of the
leafy covering. The white, or faintly-green-white of
the thick and fleshy leaf-stalk, and the crumpled
surface of the leafy portion—as yet, in the incipient leaves we are examining, not fully expanded
—would be noticed by the least observant: but
the tiny leaf deserves a closer examination.
Looking at it with a glass, one is struck by the
symmetrical regularity of the entire under-surface
of stalk and stem, or midvein, and of the veins
which branch from it.   The crumpled, leafy edge
is bent under, all round.   What is especially
noticeable, is the prominent way in which, in the
under-surfaces of the leaves, the veins stand out,
and, crossing and interlacing each other, leave
distinct hollows or depressions, the spaces between
which are densely clothed, as well as are the rib-

ELM.

like veins and veinlets, with white downy hairs. It
is this hair which gives the white and mealy or
cottony appearance to the underside of the leaf
of the Primrose. The spaces between the veins
and veinlets, concave on the underside of the leaf
are convex on the upper side, and serve to give
its crumpled appearance to the upper surface of
the leaf. The down glistens as the light catches
it. Down is also spread along the upper side
of the midstem, and shorter and smaller downy
hairs are spread upon the upper leafy side. Even
a tiny, incipient leaf of Primrose, no more than
three-quarters of an inch long, is, in mid-Winter,
a thing of beauty.

Too wide in its wealth of verdancy is the world
of wintry greenness to have detailed mention in
these pages. How many of the plants that in
spring and summer display the gorgeousness
of blossom have persistent foliage of freshest
green during the 'dead' season, only those
know who know the wintry lanes and meads and
moors and woods ; and, descending to the world
of cryptogamic vegetation, there are regions on
regions clothed with graceful ferns and moss and

lichen.   Earth-bank, rock and wall, stream-side,
foot path, roadway, the woody forest, the open
moor or heath, cliffs and beach by the seaside, the
rocky valley, the mountain, the level field, nay,
the water itself, both the briny sea and the fresh
river, stream, or brooklet,—all furnish their quota
of perennial greenness to brighten the aspect of
Winter.

V.

EEN though the wind may blow, and desolate as may be the out-look from warm habitable rooms upon fallen snow, there is, nevertheless, more than a charm, there is a strange fascination, in a snow-storm. Who has not felt this charm and experienced this fascination when looking at the operation of one of the most silent, yet one of the most beautiful of the forces of Nature?   In the *sounds* of Nature, there is much to impress our sense of hearing. There are few amongst us, probably, who do not experience a feeling of awe at the sudden crash of thunder with its accompanying reverberations;

G 2

at the mighty roar of a cataract; or at the heavy
impact of a furious sea upon a rock-bound coast.
Other sounds there are in Nature which impress
or charm us in a degree determined by the *force*
of the operations which give rise to them. The
impetuous rush of flood-water along the bed of a
mountain stream; the whistling and moaning of
the wind as it moves with a strength which sways
to and fro the giant forms of trees; the beating
of heavy rain, and the hiss of a hail-storm. Or the
dreamy gurgle of a trickling stream; the summer
breeze discoursing leafy music amidst the foliage
of a wood, and the soft sounds of bird and insect
life. In her sights, too, Nature can appal or
charm, as the mood befits her—appal by the lurid
outburst of a volcano carrying death far and wide
to the animal and to the plant world; by the flash
of the electric fluid charged with death to all
living things which may lie in its irresistible path
to the earth, and by the blaze of fire which has
won the mastery over human efforts at repression
—and she can charm by the golden or silvery
light of sun or moon; by the beauty of form and
by the wealth of varying colour.

With falling snow there is no audible sound, and perhaps one of the greatest charms of this especial operation of Nature is its noiselessness. There is something indescribably beautiful and graceful in the descent of the feathery flakes of purest white as they come, thick and fast, upon every level surface and upon every ' coign of vantage.' The process begins and continues in silence—continuing oftentimes with such per- sistence as to suspend human operations by blocking up the artificial channels of communi- cation established by industrial populations ; and the smallness, the lightness, and the adhesiveness of the individual particles which compose a snow- storm, enable fallen snow to assume the pictu- resqueness which lends so attractive an aspect to our Winters. But irregularity of the surface on which the snow falls is essential, in order to produce this picturesqueness—produced by the presence of snow on the landscape—picturesque- ness, we mean, in an external degree, for as we shall see anon, apart from their effect as a whole, individual snowflakes have each an intrinsic beauty and interest. A level ground is soon covered with a white mantle by rapidly-falling flakes. But on a broken surface the points and angles presented by jutting corners of earth, stone, or rock, and by the stems and twigs of the leafless shrubs which may be growing around, first catch the airy, feathery particles of crystallized moisture, and display the beauty of their whiteness by contrasts of colour—the sombre colour of rock and earth, of the brown bark of leafless shrubs, or of Winter evergreens. Ere long, however, the persistence of a snow-storm will cover all lowly objects, and drape the earth with a thick and level carpet of white. But above this level uniformity of whiteness, trees will still lift their beautiful heads and present the especial charm and picturesqueness of snow-clad sylvan Winter.

And how softly and gracefully is the sylvan panorama produced, and how deftly the work is done! If the wind stirs not to spoil the process, what marvellous fabrics of beauty are built upon every twig! In ten thousand corners and angles, produced by the extensive ramification of a tree, the white crystalline objects are piled in profusion.

It has all the appearance of veritable fairy-work. Upon the substantial basis afforded by the fork, where the limbs first part from the trunk, or, above, where thick branches and boughs divide from the limbs, it is not surprising to find snow crystals piled in abundance. But the process is continued by gradation upwards—higher and higher—for the tiniest sprigs and the tiniest of sprays support their burdens of flakes, raised upon the most slender of foundations, each snow-crystal clinging to each and forming structures of singular delicacy and beauty, the countless variations of which render detailed description impossible, but give the mind impressions that stimulate the sense of wonder and arouse admiration in the least emotional beings.

The picturesque and beautiful effects of fallen snow vary with the variation in the arboreal forms on which it is displayed, and when different species of trees and shrubs grow side by side, the contrast is most marked and striking. Evergreens strike the eye most by contrast of colour; deciduous trees, stripped, as they are in winter, of their leafy appendages, by the beauty of form.

In the rigid Holly the snow is caught at a thousand points by the curled and prickly leaves, and though the freight be heavy, the tree stands erect and firm, its dark-green colour showing vividly out from the folds of its crystalline mantle. In the broader-leaved Laurel, a larger, yet softer and more pliant foundation is provided, and the stems are often bent to the ground under their superincumbent weight. Yet still some spots of green are left to set off in contrast the white, enveloping shroud; and numberless evergreens, ranging in the size and texture of their leaves from extremes to intermediate forms, give rise to almost countless variations in their snow-storm spectacle.

But it is upon the naked forms of trees that the snow-crystals are displayed with the most striking effects; for the flakes adhere more readily to the rougher surfaces of the leafless twigs and branches than to the more or less smooth and glossy sides of leaves. The absence of foliage exposes to the influence of the white, fairy-like enchantment tens of thousands of little points of vantage; and beautiful as at all times is the ramification of a tree when seen in its full perfection, as it is in the Winter, it is exceptionally beautiful when the numberless and elegantly disposed limbs, branches, twigs and spray are emphasized, so to speak, by the presence of the pure and brilliant substance that sets them off.

From our brief and hasty consideration of the beauty of snow, let us pass to its utility. How often, before the advent of frost—hard biting, all-destroying frost—that, unchecked and unresisted, would press life out of the vegetable world, has Nature gently and softly and noiselessly sent the white, all-enveloping mantle of snow to keep warmth, and, with warmth, life, in the atmosphere which most closely and immediately invests the plant regions. Cold and icy as it is to the touch, it is nevertheless a most effectual garment; for, as we know, our clothes do not actually warm us, but only keep in close contact with our bodies the warmth which the latter radiate; so the snow, intensely cold as, in itself, it is, keeps in and around the plants it covers, both the heat which they themselves give off, and the heat which is radiated from the ground beneath them.

VI.

TRANGELY beautiful was the prospect we looked out upon in the morning from our forest lodging ! Snow had silently fallen during the night, and had flung its fairy mantle far and wide upon the landscape. For a moment the nearer view engrossed our attention. By our window rose an ivy-mantled Spruce, whose sweeping, pendant, outward branches alone had caught the snow, which hung from them like large, white hands, with fingers spread and pointing downwards. Below it on the right spread and drooped the twisted, picturesque branches of an Apple-tree, on the upper side of which—on every limb, bough, and twig—was strewn the crystal whiteness. The air was motionless, no wind having stirred to shake the marvellous fabric. And hence the reason why the clustered snow-flakes had poised themselves upon the highest, upright points of twigs, gathering there into small white balls.

But now, lifting our eyes forest-wards, we take in, as the vision ranges over the distant stretch of spreading woods, a scene of gathering splendour. The foreground forms of Oak and Beech for a moment attract attention to the rimy beauty of their wintry boughs and twigs; but looking on-wards and outwards, where the woods rise one over the other, our admiration culminates in the magnificent prospect which is afforded by the mass of snow-covered branches, presenting—though so distant—not a confused glare of white, but an appearance as of a vast sheet of fairy-like fret-work, like that which would be produced if a mist which had been hanging in the air and obscuring the tree-heads from view had suddenly been condensed and precipitated on the forest, leaving clear the atmosphere above it, so that the eye might, without impediment to the vision, take in the whole of the beautiful prospect.

As we have been looking, however, the sky has darkened threateningly, and a shadow has crept over the forest, obscuring the beauty of the distant fretwork. The reason of this change soon becomes manifest, for the air is presently filled with great, falling flakes, floating with silent beauty to the earth, and, though obscuring the sylvan prospect on which the eye had been delightedly looking, giving new loveliness to the nearer scene.

VII.

HE next scene is a city and suburban one; the city is London, and the suburbs and environs the country towards Boxhill. Passing over London Bridge after a snow-storm, the short period since the fall had sufficed to turn the crowded roadway and footways into mud, so enormous was the noisy traffic of vehicles and foot-passengers. The big river, too, beneath the arches of the bridge was busy with traffic, but wharf-roofs lining its banks and many a boat and other vessel were white with vestiges of the storm. Taking train from London Bridge station for

Boxhill, we are soon out of the hurly-burly.
On many housetops, in the six-foot ways, and in
many a suburban garden, as we rapidly pass on-
wards, the precipitated whiteness is conspicuous.
The snow gradually gains ground as we come
upon meadows and trees outside the great city.
By Champion Hill, Tulse Hill, and Streatham,
passing in alternation level stretches of line and
snow-covered embankments, the white expanse of
meadows, the picturesque forms of snow-clad
Oaks, and undulating enclosures of fields and
trees. From Streatham to Mitcham Junction by
the leafless forms of Elms bordering meadows,
the delicate branches of the trees prettily whitened
here and there. Then along the edge of a grassy,
furzy common, and on to Hackbridge. From
Hackbridge to Carshalton, whose houses are scattered amidst its snow-tipped trees; on, by limestone cuttings, to Sutton. From Sutton by snowy,
spreading fields to Cheam. Here let us pause a
moment to remark that the genial author of
' Forest Scenery ' lived at Cheam from 1752 to
1777. He became, first, principal assistant, and
then master, at a school in that village. It was

there that he married, and from that starting-place that he made those tours through England, Scotland, and Wales that formed the foundation for his various books on 'Picturesque Beauty,' which were all written and published during his residence there, except 'Forest Scenery,' which was conceived, written, and published during his residence at Boldre, in the New Forest. We shall, we trust, be forgiven for this digression! Past Cheam the route is through undulating country—cultivated, but now snow-covered, fields, studded here and there with the wintry, snowy forms of trees—to Ewell. From thence it is not a long journey to Epsom, partly embowered in trees, by a furze-covered embankment and through a furzy common, and away to Ashstead. Through more undulating country, with distant views of snow-clad hills, to Leatherhead. The way now becomes bolder, the tree-covered hills take rounder sweeps; we are hurried from the snowy landscape into the dark depths of a tunnel, and, reaching anon its other side, emerge amidst the beautiful scenery of Boxhill.

From the station we take a turn round to the

right into a road which, as we follow it, winds round to the left, and then takes a sweep round to the right. Here, just above us, now away to our right, looms the steep height of Boxhill, covered with its dark mantle of foliage. To get to the foot of the hill and commence its toilsome ascent we must cross a bridge, a peep over which induces a momentary halt. The water below is muddy and troubled by a flood, and the noise of its course is heightened by its impact against the trunk of a tree which has fallen across its course from side to side, and thus impedes the hurrying waters. A little way in front the stream is lost from view as it bends round to the right. Its right bank is margined by trees which observe no regular mode of growth, but whose mossy and lichen-covered boles are bent in different ways, some back over the stream-side meadow on the right, and some forward over the water. One tree, rooted in the bank on the right, whose roots have doubtless been loosened by the wash of the stream, has fallen forward so far that its topmost branches overhang the opposite stream-bank; another in front has its trunk wrapped in a dense

HORNBEAM.

mantle of ivy. Through the leafless branches of these trees—through the interstices between sturdy boles, twisted limbs, and the fretwork of branches, we see the dark-green and steep sides of Boxhill, flung into relief here and there by patches of snow, not melted by the sun, which is now shining brightly. But what can there be in the bridge itself worth notice on this mid-Winter day? Let us see. Looking down over one of its sides at the flowing water, there is, neverthe-less, a picture to admire. The red brick bridge-side is, in places, covered with deep-green moss in varying shades from olive to brightest emerald, and dappled with gold and crimson and orange from clustering lichen. Crossing the bridge and bending round to the right, we commence the ascent of the hill. It is a steep climb. But the climber is soon rewarded for the effort. Ere he has gone fifty yards upwards, he may turn and feel the charm of that mysterious feeling which overspreads the mind and gives a buoyant sense of nameless pleasure, as one mounts to a height from whence a view of sylvan beauty can be had over a wide-spreading landscape. If we follow the rough pathway worn by visitors on the turf which clothes Boxhill until we come to a point where the spreading Box-forest touches the path, we may then turn round and enjoy a fine sight, although the leaflessness of sylvan Winter is, from this spot, almost everywhere apparent. In the depths of the valley below, near the railway station, are a few clustered houses, the smoke from which, as we look down towards them, is slowly rising into the air. Amidst the stillness which prevails, the crow of a cock reaches us, and furnishes an audible indication of village life. Away beyond the houses, undulating country stretches—hills, with their sombre garniture of trees, rising to the right and to the left, whilst away to the west the sun is descending to the horizon formed by the crests of distant elevations. Away on the opposite side the eye can follow, in the depressions between the hills, the spreading sylvan, wintry landscape, which rolls away until it melts into a thin haze of colour. The valley between, rich with verdant beauty when held under the sway of leafy summer, is still beautiful, leafless though the trees are ; and the sounds which are thrown into especial relief by the general stillness prevailing—the sound of a passing train down below, the songs of birds, above which the blackbird and the thrush carol melodiously—are striking and impressive. But the wild Box, the line of which on the hill we have now reached, is not suggestive of mid-Winter, for it is still fresh and verdant and glossy, and in the axils of its leaves are little golden-green bunches of buds—floral precursers. Still gradually ascending we wind round over the hill to the right, and look down from that point upon the spreading country.

It is not far to the crest of the hill; but just before we reach its summit, where a seat is placed to afford both a resting-place and a point of view, we pass under the wide-extending boughs of Beeches which surround a glade on the hill-top; and here we may get a peep of sylvan beauty, rarely to be obtained. The ground on which we stand is white with snow, which covers the steeply-sloping hill-side. Just in front are shrubs of Box and Yew. On both sides of us and in front are scattered Beeches, whose trunks, limbs and

boughs are whitened by snow. The Beech-boles
are gracefully and beautifully twisted and turned,
and through a snowy, sylvan fretwork of branches
we look down upon the country below.

The sun, near its setting, is tipping the clouds
with fiery glory. The scattered snow throws
out into relief the green of the meadows and
the darker forms of leafless trees. A few
steps further on and a view from another point
over hill and valley is obtained; and then,
dipping under a green tunnel formed by over-
arching, evergreen foliage, and passing between
a Yew on one side, and a mossy-boled, mossy-
limbed and beautiful Oak on the other, with
gnarled and twisted limbs and boughs, we come
the next instant upon another outlook upon the
landscape beneath us, succeeded by yet another
through a screen formed by the wintry branches
of Beech trees, which raise their leafless heads
aloft over the dwarfer forms of Box and Yew.
By our side an Oak claims attention by the vivid
greenness and beauty of its mossy bole, silvered
by incrusting patches of lichen—by its seamed and
rugged bark, and its gnarled and twisted limbs.

Emerging now from the dense thicket of Box and of clustering trees, our path commences a descent on the other side of the hill. At this point a splendid view bursts upon us over a wide-spreading landscape; from the valley of meadow and tree down below, away to hills in the distance beyond, silvered all, far and near, by its beautiful garment of snow.

VIII.

UIESCENCE absolutely of the atmosphere is the condition precedent of the maintenance of the marvellously beautiful manifestation of nature called hoar-frost. The sudden succession of sharp frost to thick permeating fog or mist, happening in such a perfectly motionless state of the air, occasions what, but for the easy explanation of its origin, would be regarded as a curious phenomenon. We remember one such manifestation that impressed us by its singular beauty, and we took careful note of all the circumstances connected with it. The occasion was the 27th of December,

1879. A thick fog the day before had, in this case, precipitated moisture on every prominent object, on walls, on railings, on branches and twigs, on the tiniest sprays of the ramification of trees and shrubs, on blades of grass, and on the gossamer threads of spiders. The evening before, though frosty, had not been very cold, but the cold must have become greatly intensified towards the morning, and its first severe period of duration had evidently been determined by the arrival of a keen easterly wind, for everything of which the frost had taken hold, showed the hoar on its easterly side. The appearance had, therefore, a more remarkable aspect than that which usually accompanies hoar-frost, because it was more or less one-sided. It depended upon the general position of an object how the moisture had congealed upon it. One Elm tree we noted was a marvellous spectacle. Every twig was lined with a thick incrustation of ice, but in this case the icicles were on the eastern side only. Each one, too, instead of depending from or being superposed on the twig, stood out horizontally from it, and was considerably broader at its base

than at its apex, the length from base to apex
being from a half to three-quarters of an inch,
and giving to each twig the general appearance
of a small comb. The crystals were ranged,
(taking the horizontal direction from base to
apex already mentioned) in parallel lines. The
horizontal direction of these icicles was what
gave them their peculiarity, and the general effect
produced by the covering of every twig of this
large Elm in the manner described was singularly
beautiful. It was curious to note that the hoar
on each leaf or stem of the evergreens affected
by this frost took the form of the leaf or stem.
The leaf-margins of Holly and Box, for instance,
and of other evergreens were incrusted with ice
in such a way as to extend the peculiar formation
of each; and here also in some of the large
leaves of Holly the incrustation of ice was from
a half to three-quarters of an inch in breadth,
and the curious effect was witnessed of an indented
margin of ice, which, contrasting with the dark-
green colour of the Holly, looked singularly pretty.
The leaves of Box, being much smaller and more
numerous, though not serrated on their edges

and though hanging in a larger mass from the
shrub, gave a greater variety of surfaces and
presented a curiously interesting sight. The
icicles clung not only to the leaf-edges, but to
leaf-stems and twigs, and when there was any
protuberance on the stems or stalks, such as those
caused by knots from whence the buds spring,
the hoar continued the same protuberant appearance, and this fact showed the evenness and
regularity with which the process of addition by
congelation was continued. Although a good
many shrubs, both of deciduous plants and of
evergreens, were frosted all over their stems
and twigs, the majority of them were covered
with the hoar on their eastern side only. Even
the borders of turf showed the same appearance
on the side towards the east.

Here and there a large expanse of turf would
be found whitened in places where the taller
spikes of grass had been depositories of the precipitated moisture frozen on them by the keen
east wind; but along the eastern borders of such
turf the blades to a depth of some six inches
from the outer edges (next gravelled walks)

were whitened as if flour had been thickly sprinkled on them. Scotch Firs presented a very peculiar and striking appearance on account of the partial action of the frost. Whilst the greater portion of their foliage wore its normal hue of dark, bluish-green, here and there little patches of the needle-shaped leaves were frosted all over, giving an appearance like that of the silvering of the human head as years creep on. Spiders' webs everywhere were also whitened and hanging in festoons, and looked like the special decorations of a festive occasion, affording, in this instance at least, a warning to unwary flies who might, otherwise, have been entangled in the silky toils.

Of the general effect of hoar-frost, the author of 'Forest Scenery' has something to say. He remarks:—'In a light hoar-frost, before the sun and air begin to shake the powder from the trees, the wintry forest is often beautiful, and almost exhibits the effect of tufted foliage. As single objects also, trees, under this circumstance, are curious. The black branches, whose undersides are not covered with rime, often make a singular contrast with the whitened spray. Trees of minuter ramification and foliage—as the Beech, the Elm, and the Fir—appear under the circumstance to most advantage. The Ash, the Horse-Chestnut, and other plants of coarser form have no great beauty. Trees also, thus covered with hoar-frost, have sometimes, if not a picturesque, at least an uncommon effect when they appear against a lurid cloud; especially when the sun shines strongly upon them.'

IX

SNOW-FLOWERS AND ICE-CRYSTALS.

ANIFESTATIONS of Nature such as those described in the last chapter may well be termed 'festive occasions.' Yet splendid as the displays are, on account of the exquisite *arrangement* of the parts which produce such striking effects, the particles which provide the elements of the general display themselves possess a beauty which cannot be seen by him 'who runs,' but needs careful examination to properly appreciate. Beautiful as are the mere whiteness and purity of the snowy particles, their form, revealed to the curious and inquiring eye of the student of Nature, is exquisitely fashioned. To the careless observer of a snow-storm, or of a hoar-frost, nothing but white, and to him shapeless, particles are falling. Yet every particle is a crystal of definite shape, and, various as these shapes are, they all have one feature in common, for each is divided into six parts, each part proportioned with wonderful symmetry to each. Six-sided spires, each with six angles; six-sided pyramids, and six-pointed stars of varying points, some angular, some rounded. The shapes, indeed, are multitudinous, but the parts of each are exquisitely proportioned, and all are placed in exactly the same relation to each other. Of all sizes, they are some single, some double; but, whether single or double, the parts forming the additions which make up the difference of size are all added in exactly the same proportion.

A snow-flake! What is that, some reader may exclaim, but a tiny portion, shapeless and uninteresting, of snow? It is not so, however. A snow-flake is a fabric of exquisite beauty, consisting, it maybe, of one or two snow-crystals, or, it may be, of a number, of marvellous diversity of shape, as we have just shown, but all related to each other by six-sided symmetry—each part of each marvellously and accurately related.

Ice, too, whether the transparent substance that covers clear water, the heavy, semi-opaque-looking material presented to us in huge blocks, or the frail and beautiful material of which hoar-frost is made, is not a shapeless mass, but a beautiful fabric consisting of floral shapes of exquisite beauty and diversity. The same quiescence of the atmosphere needed for the most perfect form of hoar-frost must be present for the preservation of the perfection of form in snow-crystals. Should the winds roughly stir the snowy particles, and should these, when fallen, be roughly trodden under foot, their individual beauty departs, and they become shapeless masses. It is as Nature forms them that they assume the exquisitely beautiful shapes which are the admiration of all who have studied them.

Look at the ice which forms upon a pane of glass in a bedroom or sitting-room window when the frosty keenness of the external air has cooled the moisture precipitated from the interior of the room upon the glass. How exquisitely beautiful are the shapes which the crystallized icicles have assumed! Disposed are they not merely with kaleidoscopic symmetry, but with such definite and general order as to produce an appearance as of ferns or flowers. Nay, more, it is not imagination merely, but actual vision which shows these forms arrayed as trees and even as woods. There is to be found the trunk, the boughs, and the ramification of a tree, and the disposition of trees in the form of woods. Thus, therefore, microscopically, are represented much of the glory and the beauty of sylvan Winter.

X

THAWING.

NE of the most curious and interesting—for the attentive student of Nature—of the climatic influences which change the varied aspects of our sylvan landscapes, is the sudden accession of warmth, which oftentimes, in frosty mid-Winter, causes the almost magical disappearance from hill and meadow, from woodland, plain, and river-bank, and—in our towns and villages—from house-top, street, and garden, of their enveloping mantle of snow. If there be an absorbing attractiveness in the silent grandeur of the process by which Nature covers every visible object with a garment fashioned—in

FIELD MAPLE.   WILD CHERRY.

resplendent whiteness—of myriads of crystalline forms of exquisite beauty, it is scarcely less interesting to watch the sudden withdrawal of the force which gives so great a charm to the frigid cohesiveness of particles of moisture. Yet the especial charm with which the two operations of Nature to which we have referred are invested, would be lost if it were not for the existence of the plant world—of spreading tree and clustering shrub, and of the grass and other evergreen plants that cover the ground.

How beautiful is the provision for the needs of the plant world made by the presence of snow! When a period of frost, which would kill by its biting severity all growing things, is about to ensue, then the white and beautiful mantle of snow is flung over the ground to protect them from the fierceness of the cold. The cold has its mission as well as the snow, and both are necessary and act in unison. There is little warmth in the snow itself—heat in some degree there is in every body—but the looseness of the crystals as they lie together in masses renders the aggregated body of snow a bad conductor of heat, and hence the warmth which is always radiating from the earth becomes entangled in the mass, and the needful protection is afforded to living plants. But, as we have seen, it is not a coarse white mantle that is thrown over the earth, but a fabric wrought in the most exquisite form.

So soon, however, as external warmth is no longer needed, the crystalline garment is withdrawn. Its existence being dependent upon the maintenance of the degree of cold known as the freezing-point, the moment that point is passed by the slightest addition of heat to the atmosphere, at that moment the magic forms disappear, and the six-sided icy stars and other figures of beauty are resolved into the aqueous form from which, by almost a magical process, they were evolved. The process is more or less gradual. The necessary heat does not affect each individual amidst the mass of crystals at the same moment, but it is often very rapid, and the refreshing water pouring over the glistening sides of leaves which have borne the protecting crystals, cleanses them from the dust and other impurities which—deposited upon them during, perhaps, a long preceding period of dryness—would choke up their breathing pores and injure their health and vitality and vigour. As a washing, and consequently cleansing process only, the action of a thaw is oftentimes more thorough than the action of rain. From the varying angles at which leaves and stems lie, rain, even of the most persistent kind, cannot reach every point; but the moisture which precedes a hoar-frost or a snow-storm is most penetrating, and precipitates upon every exposed part of plants—trunk, branches, and twigs. Snow intervening and frost, the moisture is fixed by the formation of ice and snow crystals, and thus, when the thaw comes suddenly, every part is washed in a more effective way than could be the case by the action of rain. The earth, too, which may have been dry and parched previous to the snowfall, receives invigoration and refreshment for the roots it has to nourish by the water carried into it by the melting of snow. The plant world seems as if placed under a spell during the existence and continuance of frost and snow, and there is relief and rejoicing under the genial influence of a thaw. For those who delight, in

Winter, in that exquisite verdancy and gloss which
mark evergreens, there is perhaps no greater
enjoyment than a visit to a lane or wood, or to
any place where green life exists, immediately
after a thaw.   Everything is so delightfully fresh.
The glistening of the green foliage is like a smile
of satisfaction.   The earth and all upon it seems
to rejoice at the change.   A refreshing beverage
has been drunk : roots, stems, and leaves have
been invigorated; drying winds follow, to remove
all unnecessary moisture, and the plant world is
obviously and very materially stimulated for the
remainder of what may yet prove a trying season.
It is quite erroneous to suppose that the vegetable
world is insensible to the operations of Nature
during Winter.   Though buds swell not, and leaves
do not grow, there is an existence which is very
real, though not very obvious.   There is rest in
a large measure, but nothing at all approaching
lifelessness.   Roots are full of life and vigour,
though they may not be growing.   The subterra-
nean world of stem, root, rootlets, and root-fibres
is not subject to the same influences as the life
above ground.   To them the Winter season is by

no means dead; for them, mainly, is the snowy mantle of warmth thrown over the world, to keep them in health and security, and they feel more powerfully than the parts exposed to the light the genial influence of thawing.

XI

MIST, RAIN, AND HAIL.

AIN and hail, like snow, have for many people a fascination. There is indeed no operation of Nature that has not its interest; but the interest is doubtless proportioned to the degree of the manifestation. At its minimum, doubtless, during the progress of a slow, drizzling shower, the interest in rain—unless it chances to interfere with our pleasures or our business plans—culminates with the heavy and sudden downpour of a thunderstorm. The interference which the incident makes with human operations is probably largely accountable for the immediate attention which it secures; but apart altogether from such a personal reason for our interest, there can be no doubt that the spectacle itself is wonder-moving, when it is manifested with *force*. The sudden rattle of a violent hail-storm similarly excites not only wonder, but admiration: and this wonder and admiration are mainly, we think, attributable to the conscious or unconscious *reverence* which man feels for the works of the Almighty.

The least educated, following the commonest instincts of Nature, are attracted and their attention riveted by the violence of the elements; but mist, that noiselessly creeps over the landscape and makes its presence felt gently and insensibly, seldom occasions any wonder by its manifestations, and it requires an artistic eye and artistic feeling to appreciate the delicacy, beauty, and suggestiveness which accompany the advent of mist. Fog, which is mist intensified, has its beauty; but it is in the earlier stage of what may be called transparency that the greatest beauty is discoverable. The origin of both are well understood. Yet to many persons it would scarcely occur that fog is, in reality, nothing more than cloud, and that cloud is nothing more than fog. Those who ascend high enough on mountains to enter the region of cloud, know that the appearance is exactly the same as that of a fog. Both are fog, and both cloud—the different name merely indicating the difference of origin; cloud originating in the higher regions of the air, and fog in the lower, close against the earth. The condensation by contact of cold air currents with the moisture which is always, more or less, invisibly floating in the atmosphere, causes it to become visible, and, according to its abundance, to more or less obscure our perception of the objects between which and our sight it occurs.

The beauty caused by cloud is universally admired. The varied forms of the aerial fog, and the play of light upon it, give rise to ever-changing loveliness. The grovelling mist, however, has features of beauty which require to be seen under varying circumstances to be fully appreciated. The veil of suggestive mystery which it throws over the landscape is often delightful. The softening of glaring light, the partial obscuration of sun and moon, the hiding of detail in the larger and grander scenes of Nature where mountains and seas play their part, the soft mystery which hangs over the rush of water when hidden partially by a thin veil of obscuring moisture,—these are some of what artists call the 'effects' produced by wintry mists. As Gilpin truly says : 'Many a form and many a hue, which in the full glare of sunshine would be harsh and discordant, are melted together in harmony'—that is, under the influence of mistiness of the atmosphere. He continues: 'We often see the effects of this mode of atmosphere in various species of landscape, but it has nowhere a better effect than in the woods of a forest. Nothing appears, through mist, more beautiful than trees a little removed from the eye when they are opposed to trees at hand; for as the foliage of a tree consists of a great number of parts, the contrast is very pleasing between the varied surface of the tree at hand, and the dead, unvaried appearance of the removed one. Very often a picture in part unfinished pleases the eye more from contrast, than when every part is fully made

out.   Such, often, is the effect of the hazy medium.
The light mist is only a greater degree of haziness.   Its object is a *nearer distance*, as a *remote*
one is totally obscured by it.   In this situation
of the atmosphere, not only all the strong tints of
Nature are obscured, but all the *smaller* variations
of *form* are lost.   We look only for a general
mass of softened harmony and sober colouring,
unmarked by any strength of effect.   Sometimes
these mists are partial; and if they happen to
coincide with the composition of the landscape,
this partiality is attended with peculiar beauty.'
Gilpin adds: 'When some huge promontory
emerges from a spreading mist which hangs over
one part of it, it not only receives the advantage
of *contrast*, but it also becomes an object of *double
grandeur*.   We often see the woods of the forest
also with peculiar advantage emerging through a
mist in the same style of greatness.' *

The rapidly-moving mist, as the vapours are
chased by the wind, has also oftentimes a powerful
effect in bringing out into vivid relief certain parts
of a scene, and obscuring others, and revealing

* 'Forest Scenery,' pages 316-8.

and obscuring in alternation. Then, as Gilpin has been at pains to indicate, the contrasts are forcible between strong light illumining with brilliancy all objects it rests upon, and the indefiniteness of mistiness in parts of the same scene. In the delightful manner which makes his writings so pleasant, he describes what he indicates in the following passages. 'The effect is often pleasing when the sun rises in *unsullied brightness*, diffusing its ruddy light over the upper parts of objects, which is contrasted by the deeper shadows below; yet the effect is then only transcendant when he rises, accompanied by a train of vapours, in a misty atmosphere. Among lakes and mountains this happy accompaniment often forms the most astonishing visions; and yet, in the forest, it is nearly as great. With what delightful effect do we sometimes see the sun's disc just appear above a woody hill, or, in Shakespeare's language,—

"Stand tiptoe on the misty mountain's top,"

and dart his diverging rays through the rising vapour! The radiance, catching the tops of the trees as they hang midway upon the shaggy steep,

and touching here and there a few other prominent objects, imperceptibly mixes its ruddy
tint with the surrounding mists, setting on fire,
as it were, their upper parts, while their lower
skirts are lost in a dark mass of varied confusion,
in which trees and ground and radiance and
obscurity are all blended together. When the eye
is fortunate enough to catch the glowing instant
(for it is always a vanishing scene), it furnishes
an idea worth treasuring amongst the choicest
appearances of Nature. Mistiness alone, we
have observed, occasions a confusion in objects,
which is often picturesque; but the glory of the
vision depends on the glowing lights which are
mingled with it.'

In a thunderstorm, rain doubtless produces
its finest effect. One element of the impression
it makes is its suddenness and impetuosity. The
heavily-rushing downpour is itself picturesque,
and its accompanying incidents are striking—the
most important being the rapid accumulation of
flood-water and the powerful effect which is often
produced by it in a brief space of time. But
the silent fall has its interest and beauty. Part

of the feeling excited by gentle rain arises from associative and mental, rather than spectacular— if the expression may be used—causes. The knowledge that it is intended for a wise purpose, that it exercises a cleansing and purifying influence, that it promotes the great objects of Nature in numberless ways, produces an effect which, by insensible association of ideas, gives pleasure. Of the sensuous effects of rainfall, the freshness and coolness of the air and the temporary gloss imparted to evergreen vegetation are amongst the most important. The picturesque effects, however, are often important. Like the improvement of a drawing by a few strokes of the pencil, introducing *incidents* not previously existing, rain not unfrequently appears to emphasize the salient features of the landscape. As incidents of the rain itself worth notice, are the moderation, the acceleration, or the intermittent stopping of the storm; the parting, the brightening, or the lowering and darkening of the clouds.

Hail is much less frequent, but even more striking in its effects, though these effects are less

numerous than those caused by rain. Rain
attracts usually, but hail always *commands* attention. Both, however, are worth notice as amongst
the most interesting of the features which relieve
the 'dead' season from its undeserved reputation
for monotony.

XII.

OVELY, almost beyond expression, is moonlight. Yet there are widely differing degrees in the quality of the soft, silvery rays of the Queen of the Night as they reach us through the varying medium of the atmosphere. Their quality, indeed, is wholly determined by atmospheric conditions. Moonlight is always pleasant, suggestive, fanciful, and picturesque—whether the moon is shining with a rich red glow of colour through abounding fog: whether surrounded—as it appears to be—by a halo of glory when the air is filled with thin vapoury mists; whether sailing

—as it seems to do to our vision—through a sea of silver-tipped clouds, or standing out unrelieved against the clear blue vault of the sky. But of all the aspects under which moonlight can be seen, there is none, we think, which has the especial splendour of display in the same degree as that which is produced by the moon in a spotless sky, with atmospheric conditions of absolute clearness and purity. Such conditions exist in many seasons of the year, but perhaps seldom does the moon shine with such exceptional brilliancy as into the clear, frosty atmosphere of a Winter night. It is probably the greater steadfastness of the light in Winter that gives the impression of greater beauty or of a greater extreme of intensity. In the summer woodlands there is always more or less of motion; for breezes, imperceptible to the keenest sense of touch, move the fragile, mobile leaves of deciduous trees. If we do not see the leaves move, we can see the motion of their shadows, whether cast by sun or moon; and with motion there is *sound*—it may be barely audible, but there is sound. If the nightingale is not pouring forth his melody into the woods, there

PLANE.   (A FROSTY MORNING.)   ELMS.   LOMBARDY POPLAR.

are other sounds of bird or insect. Night moths, too, though their flitting be noiseless, attract attention by their *motion*, and distract the eye sensibly, though it may be unconsciously, from the brilliancy of light. But in Winter the birds are silent; no insect form flits between the eye and the landscape; leaves, even of evergreens, in the stillness of the frosty air, make no audible sound; even the shadows of boughs and spray move not, and the brilliant moon, shining in full-orbed splendour in a cloudless sky, sheds a brilliancy which *absorbs* attention. Hence it is that Winter moonlight gives impressions of exceptional beauty when the orb of night rules in silent majesty.

But clouds, sound, and motion—as *incidents*—give their varying interest to Winter moonlight. Perhaps a railway journey affords one of the most rapid means of estimating the changes of moonlight, and the variety of the circumstances which promote or are promoted by these changes. Here is a typical scene.

The journey is commenced in darkness, relieved only by lights twinkling amongst trees from cottages by the way. Then the full moon first peeps above the horizon, and soon emerges into full view, casting as yet but a feeble light. Anon, it struggles through fleecy clouds, now appearing, now obscured. Then at length it rises clear into the blue arc, throwing the full flood of its silvery radiance upon meadow and hedge and tree. The wintry trees have an appearance of singular stillness, of desolateness and abandonment—for in summer, when clothed with their delightful dress of green leaves, there is about them an air of comfort, a sort of restful fullness.

Here and there meadows which receive the full light of the moon are thrown into relief by the shadows which lurk in trenches that cross and intersect them. Presently the vision momentarily changes as the train runs into a station. The red, blue, and white lights; the sheen of the worn and polished rails as the moonbeams are reflected from them; the rush of passengers for refreshment; the hurry, bustle, and general excitement; the lights of the town, sometimes houses only, and sometimes houses and trees—sometimes level, and sometimes undulated or hilly. Then away again into a country, it may be of moonlit fields and woods, or of a sparsely-inhabited region, where the twinkle of scattered lights gives a human interest to the scene.

Now the eye is attracted by the different forms of the spray, whether of tree or bush, exposed in its wintry beauty; now by the white walls of house or farm building; now by the still forms of cattle or sheep, in harmony both with the scene and with its silence. The shadows of the taller trees, thrown by the moon in its early rising, are so long that they stretch almost across the meadows—shadows broad or narrow, according to the size of the tree-heads. Whenever clear water is passed, it brilliantly reflects the moonlight, and flashes like molten silver; when it fills the intersecting trenches of meadows, its effect is often striking—the grassy swards being thrown up in strong relief against the silver flash of the water. The effect is greatest where the streams of water are broad; and when these are running, the appearance is like that of liquid silver in motion. A great solemnity seems to rest upon the Elms, standing in the hedges in silent leafless rows or in groups.

K 2

As it approaches the zenith, the moon gains in impressiveness, growing more bright, paling the blue of the sky, and giving beautiful and striking effects to great banks of floating cloud, which, dark in its centre, is brilliant in its silver lining. The variety in the size of clouds, too, and the various distribution of cloud masses, help to give effects of great beauty.

XIII.

 ERY beautiful are the tints of sylvan Winter. Those who say the season is ' dead ' have no eyes for its colour, life, movement, and force. 'Where is its colour?' we fancy some reader may exclaim. There is green, he will admit. How many are the shades of green? There is the dark, glistening verdancy of the Holly, and the rich depth of the Ivy. Look at Ivy glistening even from the gloom of a fog! Is it one monotonous shade of colour? No, indeed. The dark, deep glossiness of the leafy epidermis is contrasted by

tho lighter (it may be almost golden) shade of the veins and veinlets, and by the purple sheen of tho stem. Treo Ivy, with its bright and with its golden-green, mantles upon dark-brown boles and twines along bare and wintry boughs. Gorse, too, stands out in verdant lightness, Scotch Fir in its rich tinge of bluish-green, and the branches of the Yew in darker shades. Far and wide, too, spreads the mantling grass, with shades on shades of varying hue. For blue, there is the wide vault of heaven and the restless expanse of the glorious sea; for gold, the glint of sunlight, sometimes the sparkle of gorse blossoms, and always the rich colouring of incrusting lichen. Silver we look for on the Birch; crimson amidst the Holly, whose berries cling to its branches; purple in the spray of Birch and of Beech, and in the leaves and stems of tho Brambles; gold and brown together in the Bracken, and brown in the Oak and Elm, and many another stem, all varying in their shades of colour. The clouds seem to catch and gather up tho glowing tints, for though we have no green in the fleecy or piled-up masses of vapour that float under tho eye of the sun, we have the elemental rays of green in blue and yellow, and we have, too, in the clouds, fiery red, and purple, and orange, and gold.

Rich, indeed, are the wintry hues of the forest —bole, branch, spray, and foliage. Even the ground is brilliantly dyed with the deep green, the golden-green, or the purple and red, and pink and orange, and brown of moss; the red and brown of fallen leaves; and the reddish-brown of the Bracken. In meadow and lane, too, are many rich colours, unsuspected sometimes by those who have never looked for them, but often plain to the most heedless eyes. And by the sea-shore there is a wealth of beauty. Here is one little glimpse obtained during a rapid railway journey. Against the red pebbly surface of the sandstone rocks we noticed the contrast of deep green grass, and the golden blossoms of wild camomile. There had been a recent thaw, and all the colours were of the freshest. Passing meadows and trees and houses, we noted the rich colouring given on tree-trunks and walls by moss and lichen—green, and gold, and orange. Then some Scotch Firs lighted up the scene, contrasting with the bare boughs and twigs of deciduous trees by the peculiar beauty of their glaucous foliage. Even the floating weed in stagnant water seemed peculiarly rich in its vivid greenness. Upon green patches of turf peeping out of flooded meadows rooks were perched, giving relief again by their sable plumage to the colours around them.

It is the sun, however, which is the power that gives life to all the colours of forest, sea-shore, lane, or meadow. Under its inspiriting rays, gold and purple, and red and orange, the shades of brown and the shades of green, exhibit the hues which charm us by their intrinsic beauty and by the loveliness of contrast. In its absence a uniform dullness overspreads the tints we have admired; but even when the orb of day retires for a period behind masses of cloud, we often have almost a repetition of the tints momentarily withdrawn from the earth. We may not wait long for the return of the golden beams, and the intermittent play of light is in itself beautiful, for it brings in its train the variety which charms.

XIV.

EAD to a sense of things existent must be the wanderer by stream, lane, or mead, by sea-shore or through forest, who does not come back from his rambles with the feeling that there is life in Winter, though the season be 'dead.' There is much that sleeps and rests, but the pulse of life beats steadily, though somewhat less vigorously than in spring, autumn, and summer. Let him look amidst the furrowed bark of tree-boles, under the cover of evergreen leaves, amidst the blades of grass, or just under the surface of the earth, and he will find in their silk-lined cases, or suspended in their protecting hammocks, a thousand forms of insect beauty, nursed by Nature through the inclemency of the Winter; and he will find—awake and active—animal, bird, and insect life, in greater force than he ever suspected.

Movement only there is in the ever-moving breeze, giving life to stillness, moving responsive boughs and twigs, and carrying many-hued clouds across the sky. Then there is the motion downwards, downwards, of rain and hail and snow, the plash or roar of the river or torrent, the hurry of the flood, and the rush of the cataract.

Force is shown in the resistless passage of lightning, the impetuous power of stream and flood, the impact of the sea, and the overwhelming violence, or, it may be, only the gentle pressure of the wind. In all these is life, movement, and force; in all their aspects, in all their phases and degrees, in all the moods or forms in which Nature exhibits them, there is beauty.

PART II.

WINTER WOOD LORE.

WINTER WOOD LORE.

I.

SPRAY.

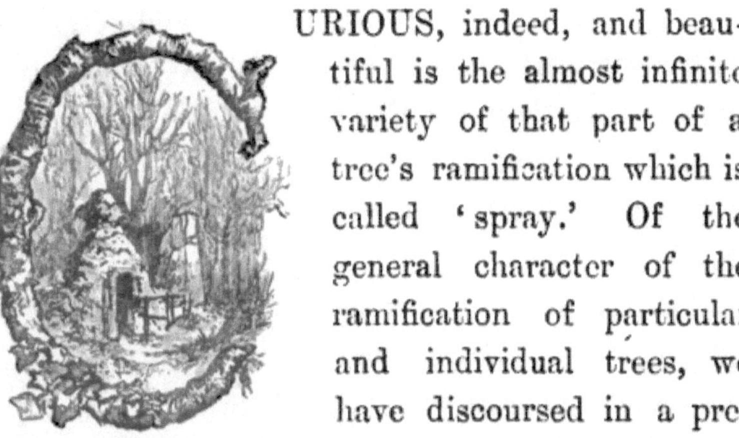

URIOUS, indeed, and beautiful is the almost infinite variety of that part of a tree's ramification which is called 'spray.' Of the general character of the ramification of particular and individual trees, we have discoursed in a previous chapter when treating of 'Tree Forms.' Here it is our object to enter into more detail, and to give to our notes and descriptions, in the text itself, that aid which is better than any other—the aid of illustrations. All have been drawn by Mr. Short from the life, and are really, not mere artistic sketches 'from memory,' but, in a sense, *facsimiles*. Gilpin rightly judged that in order to have a more accurate idea of the 'nice peculiarities and distinctions' of trees, it was essential to examine 'their smaller parts with some precision.' But he nevertheless only gave descriptions—with accompanying illustrations from drawings of his own—of the spray of four trees : the Oak, the Ash, the Elm, and the Beech.

Here we propose to greatly extend the list of subjects to illustrate and describe, but we shall borrow passages as we proceed from the descriptions given by the author of ' Forest Scenery ' of the four trees whose spray he described. Gilpin was too keen an observer not to notice how very important this study of spray was, and how much upon it depended the character of the foliage.

' Winter discovers,' he remarked, ' the nicer parts of the ramification—the little tender spray, on which the hanging of the foliage and the peculiar character of the tree so much depend. The study,' he continued, ' is certainly useful. It is true it has none of the larger parts of painting for its object—composition—or the massing of light and shade ; but we consider it as necessary for those to understand who wish either to be acquainted with the *particular character* of each tree, or its *general effect*. Nor,' he adds, ' is it an unpleasing study. There is much variety in the ramification of each species ; and much also in that of each individual. We see everywhere so many elegant lines, so much opposition, and rich intersection among them, that there are few more beautiful objects in Nature than the ramification of a tree. For myself, I am in doubt whether an old, rough, interwoven Oak, merely as a *single object*, has not as much beauty in Winter as in summer. In summer it has unquestionably more effect; but in point of simple beauty and amusement, I think I should almost prefer it in Winter. If a man were disposed to moralize, the ramification and spray of a thriving tree afford a good theme. Nothing gives a happier idea of busy life. Industry and activity pervade every part. Wherever an opening, how minute soever,

appears, there some little knot of busy adventurers
push in and form a settlement; so that the whole
is everywhere full and complete. There, too, as

Oak.

is common in all communities, are many little
elbowings, justlings, thwartings, and oppositions
in which some gain and others lose.' *

* 'Forest Scenery,' pages 136-7.

BLACK POPLAR.   LOMBARDY POPLAR.

Let us begin our description and pictorial account of the spray of trees with that of the Oak, the rugged character of which is at once shown by the illustration on page 144, which represents the stout, twisted, irregular form of the spray, the irregularity of the buds (which, though prominent, are not large for the size of the spray that bears them), and the obtuse angles at which the forking is made. There is a richness, if the expression may be used, about the very ruggedness, which is striking. The gall and the patches of lichen incrusting the lower part of the piece here drawn, indicate that the specimen was taken from a tree of some size. Gilpin—arguing that Nature seems to observe one simple principle, which is, that the mode of growth in the spray corresponds exactly with that of the larger branches, of which indeed the spray is the origin—goes on to illustrate his remarks by a reference to the Oak. He says ;—'The Oak divides his boughs from the stem more horizontally than most other deciduous trees. The spray makes exactly in miniature the same appearance. It breaks out in right angles, or in angles that are nearly so ; forming its shoots

commonly in short lines, the second year's shoot
usually taking some direction contrary to that of
the first. Thus the rudiments are laid of that
abrupt mode of ramification for which the Oak
is remarkable. When two shoots spring from
the same knot, they are commonly of unequal
length; and one with large strides generally takes
the lead. Very often also three shoots, and
sometimes four, spring from the same knot.
Hence the spray of the Oak becomes thick, close,
and interwoven; so that, at a little distance, it
has a full, rich appearance, and more of the picturesque roughness than we observe in the spray
of any other tree. The spray of the Oak also
generally springs in such directions as give its
branches that horizontal appearance which they
generally assume.'

The rich, purplish-brown colour of the bark of
the Beech twigs is at once noticeable on
examining the spray of this tree. Its gloss is
another feature observable. The buds are
irregularly produced on alternate sides of the
twigs, and the stems that produce them are of
varying lengths. The peculiar wrinkling of the

skin of the spray in places is another noticeable
feature. But the most conspicuous is the long,
slender, pointed buds in which the embryo of

Beech.

twig and leaf are carefully wrapped in their silky
cover and protected from the frosts of Winter.
The opened nut-case and the piece of lichen-

incrusted spray will be noted in our illustration.
Very pretty is the spray of the Beech, but there
is a certain angularity about the method of its
production ; the twig in continuing its course from
each node, or point of leaf-origin, does so at a
slight (very broad) angle, so that a twisting or
symmetrically zigzag appearance is given to the
spray, looked at as a whole. Gilpin remarks
that, ' the spray of the Beech observes the same
kind of alternacy as that of the Elm; but it
shoots in angles still more acute, the distance
between each twig is wider, and it forms a kind
of zigzag course. We esteem the Beech also in
some degree a pendent tree as well as the Ash;
but there is a wide difference between them. The
Ash is a light, airy tree, and its spray hangs
in elegant loose foliage; but the hanging spray
of the Beech, in old trees especially, is often
twisted and intermingled disagreeably, and has a
perplexed, matted appearance. The whole tree
gives us something of the idea of an entangled
head of bushy hair, from which, here and there,
hangs a disorderly lock; while the spray of the
Ash, like hair neither neglected nor finically nice,

has nothing squalid in it, and yet hangs in loose and easy curls.' Here, as in Gilpin's general description of the Beech, creeps in his *prejudice*—for less than such we cannot, as we have already said, regard it—against the Beech. We hold an opinion wholly different, both as regards the tree and its spray.

Very distinct and peculiar in its character is the spray of the ' Venus of the Woods.' It is the graceful aspect of the tree in its full foliage that has especially won the admiration of the poets, though, as we have previously in this volume shown, it is also graceful in its Winter undress; and its spray, too, is interesting and beautiful. More stout and rigid in aspect than that of many trees, it may not so easily win approval of those who admire graceful curves; and the prominence of its big buds may also similarly take from its appreciation. But surely the skin of a ' Venus ' is an important element of beauty, and the ashen-grey skin of the Ash is very beautiful, and there is a rich rotundity in what may be called its ' mouldings,' which must please the ' picturesque eye.' Gilpin, in comparing the spray of the Ash

next after that of the Oak, says : ' The spray of
the Ash is very different.   As the boughs of the
Ash are less complex, so is its spray.   Instead of
the thick intermingled bushiness which the spray

Ash.

of the Oak exhibits, that of the Ash is much more
simple, running in a kind of irregular parallels.
The main stem holds its course, forming at the
same time a beautiful sweep ; but the spray does

not divide, like that of the Oak, from the extremity of the last year's shoot, but springs from the sides of it. Two shoots spring out opposite to each other, and each pair in a contrary direction. Rarely, however, both the shoots of either side come to maturity; one of them is commonly lost as the tree increases, or at least makes no appearance in comparison with the other, which takes the lead. So that, notwithstanding this natural regularity of growth (so injurious to the beauty of the Spruce Fir and some other trees), the Ash never contracts the least disgusting formality from it. It may even receive great picturesque beauty, for sometimes the whole branch is lost as far as one of the lateral shoots, and this occasions a kind of rectangular junction, which forms a beautiful contrast with the other spray, and gives an elegant mode of hanging to the tree. This points out another difference between the spray of the Oak and that of the Ash. The spray of the Oak seldom shoots from the undersides of the branches; and it is this chiefly which keeps the branches in a horizontal form. But the spray of the Ash, often breaking out on the underside of the branch, forms very elegant pendent boughs.' *

An elegant mode of twisting distinguishes the spray of the Elm. It is stout, but abundant, the smaller shoots being short and starting sometimes at nearly right angles from the stems. The Winter buds are conical, reddish in colour, and are terminal as well as lateral on the shoots, along which they are placed in alternation.

'The branch of the Elm,' says Gilpin, 'has neither the strength nor the various abrupt twistings of the Oak, nor does it shoot so much in horizontal directions. Such also is the spray; it has a more regular appearance, not starting off at right angles, but forming its shoots more acutely with the parent branch. Neither does the spray of the Elm shoot, like that of the Ash, in regular pairs from the same knot, but in a kind of alternacy. It has generally at first a flat appearance; but as one year's shoot is added to another, it has not strength to support itself; and as the tree grows old, it often becomes pendent also, like the Ash; whereas the tough-

* 'Forest Scenery,' pages 145-6.

ness and strength of the Oak enable it to stretch
out its branches horizontally to the very last twig.

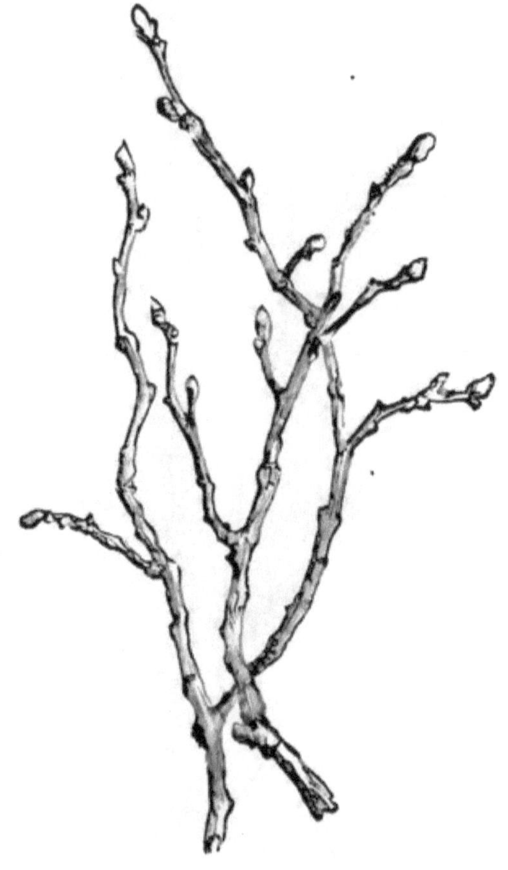

Elm.

I have seen an Oak with pendent branches, but
it is not common.' *

* 'Forest Scenery,' page 146.

Delicacy of form and beauty are, as we have already pointed out, the distinguishing features

Birch.

of the spray of the Birch, which is abundant, fine, and tapering. The purplish bark is smooth and freckled with white blotches or spots, suggestive of, and doubtless originating, the white patches that in the maturer tree adorn the trunk. The buds are conical in shape, pointed, and elegant, and from the diversion from straight lines of the shoots at each node an elegant sort of undulation is given to them. The terminal buds are very conspicuous, though small, in their dormant winter form; but their general disposition on each side in alternation occasions the elegant symmetrical appearance of the tree itself, for the graceful dependency of the branches around the trunk is arranged upon the same principle as that of the spray around the branches—for, as Gilpin remarks, ‘Nature seems to observe one simple principle, which is, that the mode of growth in the spray corresponds exactly with that of the larger branches, of which, indeed, the spray is the origin.’

Lime-tree twigs in mid-Winter are lightly and gracefully displayed, and are plentifully furnished with their red and green buds. There is a slight zigzag arrangement in the Lime twigs, which gives elegant contrast and variety to the ramification of this tree. When a bud is formed, the progressing shoot, in growing beyond it, grows away from it. Sometimes a newly-formed

Lime.

bud developes into a small twig, which may be from half an inch to six inches or more in length.

Sometimes it may only come into a leaf, and it is the variation in length of the shoots that gives a beautiful irregularity to the ramification. Even in icy mid-Winter the buds are beautifully bright and glossy and fresh—green oftentimes on one side, and red on the other. The ends of the previous year's twigs are often of a green or of an olive-green colour. A cut across such twigs exhibits the soft green inner bark surrounding the cylindrical column of white tissue, which, in its turn, surrounds the long cylinder of white pith. A magnifying-glass will show that there is plenty of sap in the twig, for the tissue glistens as the light falls upon it. If we cut across the red-green bud, we shall see inside its scales the incipient verdant leaf, enfolded within the covering in such a way as to exemplify the greatest possible economy of space. There the tender embryo leaf waits only for the first touch of spring to start into vigorous life. Though appearing to be wrapped in only a single scale, the Lime-bud envelope really consists of several scales, and by the side of each bud appears a smaller one, ensconced in the same covering.

In the Hornbeam it is noticeable that the buds of the spray are produced, not on alternate sides,

Hornbeam.

but all around the shoots. They are conical in shape, the shoots are small, and the bark with which they are clothed is of a reddish colour.

The general aspect of the spray is, like that of the tree as a whole, contorted and horny.

The bark of the shoots of the Field Maple is

Maple.

brown in colour and striated, dull and rough. The shoots are somewhat stout, and the branches which produce them twisted and irregular. The

nodes appear at irregular distances along the
stems or twigs, and are blunt-shaped and somewhat conical, as well as being terminal. The
shoots are produced, mostly, nearly at right

Sycamore.

angles from the stems which bear them. In
colour the bark is reddish, but the general appearance of the ramification is rugged.

ABELE POPLAR.

Sycamore shoots show the same winter life as those of the Lime and of some other trees; but the buds are larger and are wrapped in several somewhat oval-shaped, over-lapping scales. Within these, fresh and green and full of vigour, though sleeping, is the beautiful, incipient form of the future green leaf, wrapped round and round upon itself. The bark of the Sycamore shoots may be described as being reddish-grey in colour. The buds on the shoots are produced in pairs along them, and they are also terminal, large, and conical. Beneath each bud the bark is curiously wrinkled, and the general character of the shoots is robust.

On the smaller branches of the Larch the bark is a very light shade of brown; on the larger ones, such as that shown in the accompanying illustration, it is darker in its hue of brown. In his drawing of the spray of the Larch our artist has given us some rugged bits of shoots, with a couple of empty cones and some incrusting lichen. The buds are numerous and rounded, and are produced all round the stems. The branching of the shoots from the main stem is at obtuse

angles.   When first produced, the spray of the
Larch is very symmetrical, the shoots being arranged all round the stem in alternation in a

Larch.

very symmetrical manner, as we have shown in
discussing the tree as a whole.

Of the zigzag and eminently picturesque

character of the ramification of the Plane we
have spoken in a previous chapter, when dealing
with the forms of trees. The same character, it

Plane.

will be seen, distinguishes the spray of this tree,
as shown in the drawing. The bark of the shoots
of the Plane is greyish, with white freckles. The

buds are produced irregularly along the twigs,
but mostly in opposite alternation. It is this
arrangement which occasions the picturesqueness
of growth of this tree, taken in connection with
the manner of growth of the shoot from node
to node. Sometimes, as will be noticed by our
drawing, the shoot in growing beyond the node
grows straight, and sometimes it grows at a more
or less sharp angle from it, thus causing the
turns—which are more or less sharp in degree—and
the angles, which are sometimes acute and sometimes broad. The buds of the spray are not very
prominent, though sufficiently conspicuous both
at the nodes and at the ends of the shoots. They
would be more conspicuous but for a beautiful
provision of Nature by which the tender embryo
leaf, enclosed within the outer covering, is protected from frost and cold. The leaf-stalk of
the Plane is hollow at its base, and under this
hollow part is found the new bud. When the
leaf drops in the fall of the year, the bud for the
next season is revealed, but the covering it loses
by the fall of the protecting hollow of the old leaf-
stalk has been very beautifully provided for.

Over the bud itself there is a silky covering; upon this, soft, hairy scales; and over all a resinous case, perfectly wet-proof. Discoloured by exposure to the air, one would naturally regard this external appearance as the bud; but the bud, composed of delicate and tender tissue, lies within, safe against all the bleakness of the wintry season.

Almost every winter bud has some such provision as this for its safety, but there is an especially elaborate and beautiful provision made for the safety of the Plane bud. Nature works in a more or less elaborate manner, according to the more or less important objects she has to secure, and the purpose of the especial provision made for the leaf of the Plane may be readily divined by remembering the large size and the exquisite beauty of the summer foliage of this delightful tree.

The spray of the Poplar differs in the various species of that most abundant tree, but in the spray of all the species the bark is more or less brown in colour, and there is much straightness and symmetry in the growth of the shoots, thus marking the absence of the zigzag angularity which gives so peculiar a feature to some other trees. Taking four of the species we may indicate the distinguishing characters. In the Black

Poplar.

Poplar (*Populus nigra*) the spray is greyish-brown, stout, somewhat rough, and furrowed or ridged; the branching intermediate and irregular; the buds numerous, produced all round the stems, conical, and pale red in colour—the little shoots of the spray being from half an inch to an inch in length. In the Grey Poplar (*Populus canescens*) the bark is smooth to the touch, and brownish-grey in colour; the buds are small, terminal, conical, and reddish-coloured; and the spray stout, and much-divided, the ends pointing upwards symmetrically, and the conical form of the whole resembling that of the Lombardy Poplar. The bark of the spray of the Abele Poplar (*Populus alba*) is smooth, and light grey in colour; the buds are all round the shoots, conical and red-tipped, terminal, and small in size; and finally, in the Lombardy Poplar, the bark of the spray is smooth in texture and light brownish-grey in colour, and the spray is much inclined upwards, the angle at which it leaves the shoots being very acute, and the buds small, abundant, and blunt in form.

Their wintry greenness is perhaps, joined to the smoothness and glossiness of the bark, the most noticeable feature of the spray of the Willow. Upon the bark is also, oftentimes, found splashes of reddish-brown. In all the Willows the grading of the shoots from base to apex is very symmetrical, and the buds are noticeable by their tongue-shaped form and by their cleaving to the shoots,

Willow.

though they are generally small and inconspicuous. They are produced all around the shoots, and thus it is with this tree, as in the case of others whose buds are produced in this way, that a very regular appearance is given to the ramification as a whole, because that bushiness is produced which Gilpin admired, the fillings up and jostlings of the twigs one with another, that give so good an emblem of 'busy life.' In the Willow, in what in respect to other trees we regard as mid-Winter, we shall notice that sign of life which is exhibited by the flowering. Though a wintry manifestation, the spectacle really indicates the 'Willow's' spring; but, howsoever we regard it, the appearance is a beautiful one.

There is decided 'character,' it will be admitted, in the shoots of the Chestnut. The bark is a rich, dark, glossy brown, prettily freckled with white, suggestive of the handsome Hazel skin. The buds are irregular, as is also the spray, and those which terminate the shoots are very prominent and large, as indeed is necessary, regard being had to the ample size of the handsome leaf which is folded up within this close and frost-proof covering. The reader with some imagination, in looking at our illustration of Chestnut spray, will perhaps fancy he sees some resemblance to the foreleg and hoof of a horse, and will, we think, admit at any rate that this spray does, as we have premised, exhibit ' character.'

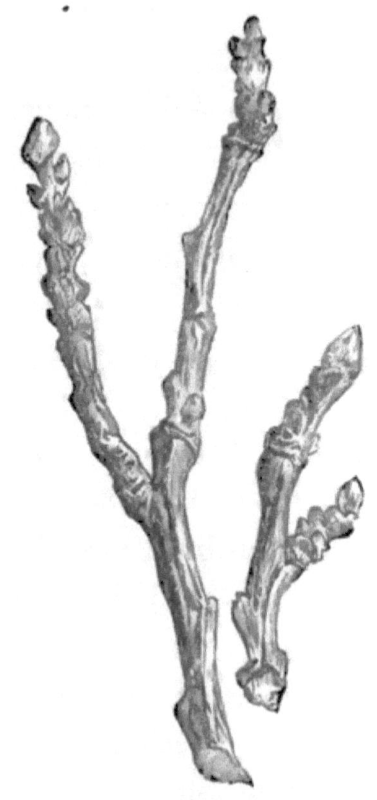

Chestnut.

From the Chestnut to the Horse Chestnut, though the trees are not related, may perhaps, regard being had for popular fancy and association, be considered a fitting succession. Especially stout and vigorous is the spray, whilst the buds are very large. Our artist has well shown

Horse Chestnut.

both the stoutness of the shoots and the largeness of the buds of the Horse Chestnut, whilst elsewhere we have shown the peculiar character of the ramification. That the winter buds should be so large will not occasion any surprise, when it is stated that each bud contains in embryo, not

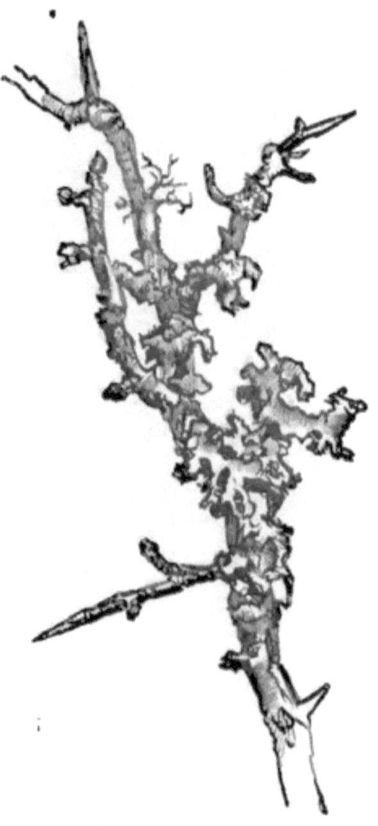

Lichen-covered Hawthorn.

merely one large leaf of the following season, but a whole shoot, with several leaves and flowers.

A lichen-incrusted, thorny, and picturesque specimen of the spray of the Hawthorn will give an idea of the picturesque, contorted beauty of this delightful shrub or tree, as it frequently becomes, when fully grown. Twisted and picturesque, even the youngest spray becomes, and then it is overspread by a purple hue, which produces a fine effect of colour when masses of it are seen in Winter; but when it has reached maturity, it becomes striking and grand in the contortion of its beauty. The bright red berries, too, clinging to the shoots long after the leaves have fallen, give a charm to its Winter form, which, empurpled by the pervading colour of the spray, stands out in great richness.

The ruggedness of the spray of the Apple is its most prominent and picturesque characteristic. Stout, thick, and rough, the bark wrinkled and lichen-covered, the ramification proceeding at all sorts of angles and producing shoots of all sorts of lengths, tipped each with the substantial-looking bud, that, embrowned and dead-looking, nevertheless encloses branch, leaf, and fruit for the succeeding season, the twig of Apple is a thing of interest. Our artist's illustration is taken from the spray of the wild species, the well-known 'Crab Apple,' whose fruit, though sour to the taste, is beautiful to the eye; and whose form is full of

Crab Apple.

interest and picturesqueness. The art of the gardener has transformed the descendants of this forest inhabitant into a thousand forms of utility,

which are curious departures from the parental
or ancestral form, so far as their fruit is concerned; but the spray, whose wintry character
we are now considering, has in all the varieties,
through all modifications, preserved much of the
especial interest and charm which distinguish the
hereditary 'Crab.'

Lost as it would otherwise be amidst the
tangled growths of the wood and the hedge, the
Hazel is noticeable by the splashed and freckled
character of its smooth and shining bark, as well
as by its mid-Winter show of 'catkins.' The
spray in its mode of ramification is not unlike
that of the Elm, the buds being placed on
alternate sides of the shoots, and the continuation
of the latter diverging at each node out of a
straight line, and at what may be called a broad
angle; the buds also in form suggesting those
of the Elm. But there is much greater irregularity in the spray of the Hazel than in that
of the Elm, a disposition to proceed on the principle of 'filling up' every little vacuity, without
regard to symmetry. Hence it is, doubtless, that
the shade of the Hazel in summer is so dense, as

the leafy shroud, following the lead of the ramification, fills every space.

Hazel.

The never-ceasing brook goes singing on in
Winter as in summer, and far louder oftentimes

ACACIA.

in the former season, so that its music will attract us to the presence of the wintry Alder. Gilpin loved the Alder, though his praise of it had chiefly

Alder.

reference to its foliaged condition. Comparing another waterside tree—the Willow—with the Alder, he thought that the latter was 'the more picturesque tree, both in its ramification and in its foliage. Perhaps,' he added, 'it is the most picturesque of any of the aquatic tribe, except the Weeping Willow. He who would see the Alder in perfection,' he continued, 'must follow the banks of the Mole in Surrey, through the sweet vales of Dorking and Mickleham, into the groves of Esher. The Mole indeed is far from being a beautiful river; it is a silent and sluggish stream. But what beauty it has it owes greatly to the Alder, which everywhere fringes its meadows, and in many places forms pleasing scenes, especially in the vale between Box Hill and the high ground of Norbury Park.' There is a ruggedness about the spray, as our illustration will show, that quite accounts for the picturesqueness of the shrub or tree—for the Alder is both, according to its more or less favourable conditions of growth. The winter buds are prominent, and the shoots are irregularly produced, and grow irregularly, thus giving rise to that 'picturesqueness' which inequality of growth often causes.

'Character' we may again claim for the form

of spray in the case of the Mountain Ash. Its
young shoots add to the smoothness and sym-

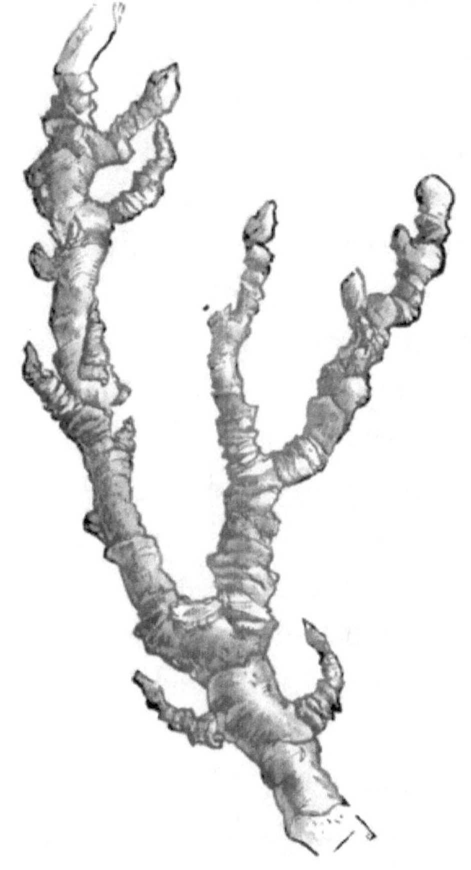

Mountain Ash.

metry of their form a beautiful purplish and
frecklcd condition. Buds are produced all around

the shoots, and are conical and prominent, dark-coloured and terminal. As the tree acquires size and age, there supervenes a rich, crumpled appearance, which, as our engraving shows, gives to it the 'character' we have already claimed for it. Without, there is a smoothness of bark suggestive of the Beech, and a lightness of hue in the 'larger parts,' which, combined with the smoothness, is beautiful.

'In ancient days, when superstition held that place in society which dissipation and impiety now hold,' sternly remarked Gilpin, 'the Mountain Ash was considered an object of great veneration. Often at this day a stump of it is found in some old burying-place, or near the circle of a Druid temple, whose rites it formerly invested with its sacred shade. Its chief merit now consists in being the ornament of landscape.' He continues, 'In the Scottish islands it becomes a considerable tree. There are some rocky mountains covered with dark Pines and waving Birch, which cast a solemn gloom over the lake below; a few Mountain Ashes joining in a clump, and mixing with them, have a fine effect.

In summer the light-green tint of their foliage, and in autumn the glowing berries which hang clustering upon them, contrast beautifully with the deeper green of the Pines; and if they are happily blended, and not in too large a proportion, they add some of the most picturesque furniture with which the sides of these rugged mountains are invested.' *

The lightness of the pinnate foliage of the Mountain Ash does not adorn the wintry landscape, but another contrast with the dark-green hue of the Pine is furnished by the absence of leaves and the presence oftentimes of red berries, which enkindle the twigs, bared of their summer dress—so that still the tree is beautiful and striking.

The prickly Blackthorn must not be forgotten in our enumeration of the spray of trees. Commonly seen as a bush, it often becomes a not inconsiderable tree. Twisted, bent, irregular in its growth and sharply spined, the spray of this common but interesting plant is worth notice. Cultivation and domestication have largely de-

* ' Forest Scenery,' page 59.

prived the Plum, which is the descendant of the Sloe, of its thorny mail.   In the rougher habitats of the forest it is armed to the teeth, as our en-

Blackthorn.

graving will show—so stoutly armed indeed is it, that the thorn often continues in a straight line the twig which bears it and gives the appearance of a spear, whilst the lichen-incrusted stems and the

purplish bark combine to invest it in a high
degree with the character of picturesqueness.

Beautiful unquestionably in its mid-Winter guise
is the spray of the Yew, with the reddish-brown

Yew.

tinge of the shoots and the dark-green glossy
leaves. But of this tree and of its characteristics
we have spoken amply elsewhere, as we also have
of the Scotch Pine. So let us merely be content

to give two little sketches of the spray of each as
a suggestion to those who may wish to give more
detailed attention to the study of the ' minuter

Scotch Fir.

parts' of these two interesting and delightful
trees.

With an engraving of, and a brief reference to, the spray of the Cedar of Lebanon, our illustrations of 'spray' will be concluded. Pretty and

Cedar of Lebanon.

striking in its bunchiness, if the expression may be used, is the needle foliage of this beautiful evergreen. The leaves, like those of the Larch,

which has been called a deciduous Cedar, are produced in tufts, or little bunches, from the shoots,
and even in winter are very beautiful in their
verdant freshness. There is a roughness and
ruggedness about the bark of the twigs which, in
conjunction with the colour of the foliage, gives a
very picturesque character to the spray of this
noble tree.

II.

TILITY is, in reality, too negative an expression to apply to the purposes to which the wood of trees is devoted. 'Indispensability' would be a far more appropriate word. A moment's reflection will show us the entire dependency of the world upon the products of the forest; and it is impossible to imagine what would have become of mankind but for the aid, sustenance, and support, the comfort, well-being, and happiness promoted by the existence of timber. The fact, however, that we daily and hourly walk in it, take shelter under it,

and handle it in some form or another, does not of
itself explain much as to the nature and particular
purposes of particular kinds.   The universally
generic expression 'wood,' or 'timber,' goes
a long way towards satisfaction; but the dis-
crimination of the different kinds used for the
varying purposes of civilization is not a general
possession; it is mostly the possession of experts.
Yet the subject is one, we think, of interest, and
in the immediately succeeding pages we shall en-
deavour to furnish some data which may, and we
trust will, prove entertaining and valuable to the
general reader.   It is in this spirit that we
give the facts contained in this chapter, merely
premising that we write not for the learned
expert, but for the unlearned, and for those
anxious to be informed upon a subject, information on which has been hitherto too widely scattered
through various works to be available for ready
use.   To make the arrangement of the contents
of this chapter as convenient as possible, an
alphabetical arrangement will be followed.

Much difference of opinion exists as to the
value of the wood of the Acacia (*Robinia pseud-*

acacia).   At one time it was very highly esteemed, but of late years it has somewhat fallen into disrepute.   It is very probable that the brittleness frequently noticeable in the wood of this tree is due to imperfect conditions of growth ; and when grown under natural circumstances in soil not rich, it progresses more slowly, and does produce valuable timber.   Its general colour is a greenish-yellow, but it has brown veins.   Its qualities are hardness (which makes it susceptible of a high polish) and durability ; but it is, as we have said, brittle, owing to a lack of elasticity.   Its hardness and durability, however, make it suitable for ornaments and wooden pins, for which it is largely used, for fastening planks to beams or to the ribs of vessels.   The name tree-nail (corrupted into trenail, and pronounced trunnel) is a descriptive designation of these wood-pins.   For other purposes, when its particular qualities are desirable—such as for fences, posts, and axle-trees—it is much used.

Its waterside habitats usefully fit the Alder (*Alnus glutinosa*) for purposes for which resistance to dampness and the effects of wet is essential.

Hence for the woodwork of all structures that are continually immersed in water, such as bridges, the foundations of wharves, pumps, water-works, &c., it is invaluable.   For exposure to the weather only (which means an alternation of the wet and the dry state) it is not suitable.   But for any wood that is required to be continually buried in the earth, such as the lower parts of posts, it does well; also for wooden apparatus used for wet operations—such as bowls, kneading-troughs, sabots, clogs, and pattens—it is very serviceable. It is also used for broom-handles.   Cabinet-makers, too, employ it for manufacturing various articles of furniture.   When dyed black it is used to imitate ebony.   It makes one of the best of charcoals for the manufacture of gunpowder; and for some kinds of turning and sculpture it is also employed.   Occasionally it has fine veins, and then it is suitable for manufacturing into ornamental tables and boxes.

The familiar and useful Apple-tree (*Pyrus malus*), though abounding with beautiful fruit, also produces wood which is hard and fine-grained, and, being susceptible of a high polish, can be used for articles of fancy—walking-sticks, boxes, cases, tablets, and for things innumerable which are manufactured by the lathe for purposes of use and ornamentation. The wood of the Crab, the original stock, in its wild state has this quality of hardness and fineness of grain, and the innumerable cultivated varieties which have sprung from it retain the same qualities, a circumstance which is unusual with the wood of other trees brought into cultivation, for as cultivation generally induces a greater rapidity of growth, there is, consequently, a looseness of fibre induced that promotes softness of texture and prevents the closeness of grain which makes the most valuable quality of all timber.

From the remarkable slowness of its growth, the Araucaria (*Araucaria imbricata*) produces wood of singular solidity and hardness; but the tree in civilized countries is seldom or never grown, except for ornament, and its natural habitats are so inaccessible as to render the procuring of the wood for commercial purposes practically impossible.

Almost excelling every other tree, except the

Oak, in the wide utility of its timber, the purposes
to which the Ash (*Fraxinus excelsior*) is put are
very numerous. Its strength and elasticity combined are so great that, when employed in buildings, it will bear an enormous strain—if used for
joists—without breaking. For domestic purposes
also it is invaluable, because it does not splinter
like deal. Hence, for stairs, for kitchen tables,
even for flooring, it is a most desirable wood. In
coach-building, too, and in the manufacture of the
wooden parts of all sorts of farming and garden-
ing instruments—ploughs, harrows, and various
tools—it is invaluable, as also for hurdles, fences,
hoops of casks, crates, hop and other poles, wooden
rods, oars, fishing-rods, pulley-blocks; for carpen-
tering purposes when wood has to hold to wood
by tenons and mortises, for turning in the lathe,
for carts, ladders, and, in short, for all purposes in
which strength, lightness, and elasticity combined
are required, Ash is in great request.

Who knows that the wood of the Beech—from
its capability of being cut into very thin layers—
forms the substance of strawberry baskets? A
useful and pleasant purpose, surely, but the least

SPANISH CHESTNUT.

useful of all the varied purposes to which it is put. When green it is much harder than the wood of many other timber trees. Its whitish colour when dry and fit for use is well known, but it is not so generally known that it becomes reddish when it has been grown in good soil in level positions. For all kinds of cabinet purposes it is employed; for chairs, sometimes for tables, for bedsteads—where iron or brass has not yet superseded the old fashion—for carriage-panels, for wooden shovels, for sieve-rims, for wooden screws, and for many of the articles manufactured by the turner and the joiner, including the handles of tools, it is extensively used.

Many are the varieties of the Barberry, but we will notice only one representative—the Common Barberry (*Berberis vulgaris*). The utility of its wood, however, is not very great, though it is hard, but with its hardness it is brittle. Yet its colour, or rather the colour of its inner bark, being yellow, it produces a yellow dye, which has its use in the arts of industry.

Depending on the place of its growth, the wood of the Birch (*Betula alba*) is more or less durable—more in northern latitudes, less in temperate regions. In colour its timber is whitish, though it has a tinge of red. The bark, however, is more enduring than the wood, and is so proof against moisture that it is often bound round posts and stakes which are put into the ground, to keep them from rotting; it is also put under boots and shoes to make them damp-proof, and in parts of Europe, especially in the countries of Lapland and Sweden, where the Birch grows in abundance, the country people use it to make water-proof roofs to the cottages. A proof of the durability of the bark over the wood inside it, is given in the fact that when Birch-trees have been discovered in forests, where they have fallen and lain for a long time untouched, the wood has rotted and decayed entirely, whilst the encompassing bark has remained quite perfect and sound. In America, too, the bark is used for the construction of canoes, a striking instance of its water-proof qualities. The sheets of bark, after being stripped from the trees in lengths of about a dozen feet, by two vertical and two circular incisions—wedges being used to loosen it—are stitched at the ends with the roots of trees—those of the White Spruce are commonly employed—and the join is made water-tight by a coating of resin. Each detached cylinder of bark, cut in two, thus makes a couple of canoes, the great recommendation of which is their extreme lightness, and their adaptability for being carried across country from water-side to water-side on men's shoulders. Many persons who have not seen these canoes themselves, have seen models of them, but have not, probably, suspected that the bark of the Birch was the material employed in their construction. Amongst the uses of the wood itself, may be included its employment in making packing-cases, and wooden shoes, in turning (into articles of various kinds) and for match-making—the ease with which it splits and the rapidity of its combustion making it very useful for this last-mentioned purpose. In countries, however, where the tree largely abounds, it is often used by the population for almost all domestic and commercial purposes.

Hard wood, yellow in colour, is that of the Bird Cherry (*Cerasus padus*), and though not very

generally known as an ornamental kind, it possesses beautiful veins, and where it has grown
to a large size it is used for ornamental purposes by cabinet-makers and turners, the boards
being obtained by diagonally sawing them out
from the trees, by which means the beauty of
their markings is increased.

The extreme slowness of growth is compen-
sated for in the Box (*Buxus sempervirens*) by the
useful results which ensue—for Box is amongst
the most valuable of the timber products of the
world. Its exceptional weight is a particular feature of interest; for a cubic foot, when dry, weighs
almost sixty-nine pounds. It will, in fact, sink
in water. For a thousand and one articles of
beauty it is used by the turner and cabinet-maker.
When inlaid wood-work was more in fashion than
it now is, Box was largely used to vary the colours
of other materials; for the wood parts of mathematical, musical, and many other instruments,
and for the handles of all sorts of ornamental
things, it is still extensively used; for games, toys,
fancy boxes, cases, spoons and forks for salads,
&c.; for pins and pegs of wood, where exceptional

hardness is required; for pipes sometimes, rulers, measures, gauging instruments, wooden screws, and many other and sundry uses too numerous to mention, this beautiful wood is used. But its most valuable and important use is that made of it by the modern wood-engraver, whose beautiful and wonderful art—the reproduction of the most delicate features of Nature, and of everything which it is desired to give in the form of pictures—relies upon the exquisite susceptibility of Box to the touch of the graving tool, and upon its retentive hardness, for its success.

So seldom does the Broom (*Cytisus scoparius*) produce wood of any size for purposes of utility in the arts, that it may be interesting to mention that when it has produced 'timber,' it has been employed for similar purposes to that of the Laburnum. It has also been used for making pins for pulleys, for which purpose it was formerly said to be superior to any other wood. Certain Scotch snuff-boxes, manufactured many years since by Mr. Steven, of Laurencekirk, were made from Broom roots after the latter had been steeped in water for a considerable time.

The great value set upon the Cedar of Lebanon (*Cedrus libani*) by the ancients is indicated by the large use they made of its timber, and by the selection of it by Solomon for the wood of the Temple. Its value as timber is not so highly esteemed in the present day, though for the inferior parts of cabinets it is commonly used, and for the internal parts both of cabinets and drawers its great recommendation, in addition to its pleasant smell, is its immunity from the attacks of insects —an immunity extended also to the contents of Cedar-wood drawers and cabinets. Light red in colour, the wood may be called handsome. As it is liable to shrink and also to warp in use, its value as timber is greatly lessened.

Much superior in some respects is the beautiful *Cedrus deodara*, popularly called the Indian Cedar. The wood of this tree is compact, its grain is fine, and it is capable of taking a high polish, and, moreover, it is very durable. It is a matter of question which Cedar wood was used for the temple of Apollo at Utica, but this particular kind was found to be in a good state of preservation after two thousand years !

Reddish in colour, close-grained, and strong, the wood of the Cherry (*Cerasus vulgaris*) is much in request by turners and cabinet-makers, because it is susceptible of a fine polish, can be easily worked, and thus makes capital material for the production of handsome articles. It is, amongst other things, used for making musical instruments, and from its colour can pass muster for mahogany, or at least it has the advantage of a colour that is very much in request. In many parts of the world, where mahogany is more easily obtainable than Cherry wood, the latter would be more in request, and would be more esteemed.

Contrary to a rule that very generally holds good with regard to timber, the wood of the Chestnut (*Castanea vesca*) is better when the tree is young than when it has attained age. By about the time, therefore, that it has reached the age of fifty years, its timber is generally in a fine state of perfection. The wood of young trees is excellent at a very early stage for posts, stakes, fence-poles, trellis-work, and other purposes, for which especial durability is required. But as it acquires a greater age than that indicated, the wood gives signs of decay and loses much of its value as timber. For a long time a belief was held in England that Chestnut wood was of remarkable quality, because a good deal of it in a fine state of preservation was, it was believed, found in ancient buildings, and especially in one important building, Westminster Hall. On investigation, however, it was proved that this timber was not that of the Chestnut, but the wood of the Durmast Oak (*Quercus sessiliflora*). One curious property, at any rate, this tree possesses, namely, that of flavouring wine, for it is said that when this liquor is placed in Chestnut casks, it not only improves its colour, but its quality, and is also an aid to its preservation.

Though the Cork Tree (*Quercus suber*) is in reality an Oak, as its botanical name indicates, we put it here in our alphabetical arrangement of trees, because this seems more naturally its place. The curious thickness of the outer bark, which forms the familiar cork, lessens the diameter of the timber ; but the latter is, nevertheless, used for many of the purposes to which Oak is put, as it is very hard and heavy, and takes a high polish.

The detaching of the cork in half-cylinders—in the manner previously indicated as the method adopted for obtaining Birch bark for canoes—does not, curiously enough, injure the tree if care be taken in the process not to cut the inner bark, which in time—after the lapse of some eight or ten years—itself becomes cork, and is replaced in turn by another inner bark.

Fragrance is one special characteristic of the wood of the Common or Evergreen Cypress (*Cupressus sempervirens*). It is also hard, very close and fine in its grain, and extremely durable. It has, moreover, the advantage of colour, for it is tinged with red. Besides its hardness and great durability, it also is elastic, and thus is superior to many kinds of woods for building, both for the structural parts and for doors, stairs, and indeed for any purpose in which hardness, elasticity, and durability are requisite. In the time of Constantine it is stated that the doors of St. Peter's Church at Rome were made of Cypress wood, and when, eleven hundred years afterwards, Pope Eugenius IV. took them down, in order to erect brass ones in their places, there was no evident sign of decay—a marvellous proof of their wonderful quality. Like Cedar, the odour of the wood, though pleasant to man's taste, is objectionable to insects, and, hence, for clothes-presses it would be an invaluable material. It also, it is said, resists the attacks of worms, probably for a similar reason to that which causes insects to dislike it, and makes admirable material for any purpose which requires it to be buried in the earth. Proof of this is furnished by the fact that the cases containing the mummies of the Egyptians are commonly found to be made of Cypress. It was, perhaps, its utility in this way that suggested its employment as a funeral tree in burying-places— for even to this day the custom of employing it as an evergreen to plant over graves lingers. Itself and many of its varieties are indeed very beautiful trees, and their persistent verdure makes them very suitable for use as living memorials of the dead.

Toughness of wood is the quality which has caused its generic botanical name to be given to the genera of which the Dogwood (*Cornus sanguinea*) is the best-known species—*cornu*, a horn, suggesting the appellative designation indicative of hardness. The common name is supposed to have been suggested because the fruit is not even 'fit for a dog.' The common name of Prick-wood, an alternative of Dogwood, is much more appropriately indicative of the actual use to which the wood is put, because it is frequently made into skewers and toothpicks—more frequently into the former, as the feathered tribe (when the precious metals are not brought into requisition) furnish perhaps the largest number of toothpicks. The large numbers of spiral vessels in the woody tissue of this shrub, and sometimes tree, doubtless are largely the cause of its peculiar toughness. For other purposes than those mentioned, where especial toughness, combined with solidity of fibre, is requisite—small, pointed instruments required in the arts and manufactures, arrows, ramrods, knitting and netting needles, and meshes, &c., this wood is used and is useful. Another species of Dogwood (*Cornus mas*), the Cornel or 'Male Dogwood' (our typical species mentioned above —*sanguinea*—is sometimes called in opposition *Cornus fœmina*, the 'Lady Dogwood'), has much

harder wood, and possesses, besides its hardness—
a quality not very feminine—the qualities of toughness, flexibility, and durability. Wooden forks
used for haymaking and for other purposes of
husbandry, spokes for ladders, and hoops, as well
as toothpicks and skewers, are made from the
wood of this species; and when it is required to be
set firm in any particular shape, it is bent to the
form required, and whilst so bent is baked in an
oven, and thus fixed.

As imitation is admitted on all hands to be the
sincerest flattery, it may be assumed that the
beautiful wood called Ebony is deserving of all
the consideration that is paid to it by the manu-
facturers of the large number of materials which
are made, by the process of dressing, to do duty
for the black and heavy product of the *Diospyros
ebenus*, which is the botanical name of the true
Ebony. The difference between the true wood
and its spurious and contemptible imitations is
equal to the difference between a diamond and
paste. The term 'ebonized' has crept into use
to indicate the thousand and one articles of
furniture and articles for ornament which are

stained black to make them pass muster for the original.

Few more delicious drinks, when served warm in the depth of Winter, can be mentioned than the wine of the Elder (*Sambucus nigra*); but this beverage is mentioned here not appropriately in a discourse on woods, but only suggestively. Whilst it is well known that its leaves, blossoms, and bark possess some valuable medicinal properties, not much, perhaps, could be said for its wood, if it could only be urged that it is used for the manufacture of pop-guns and other toys— though such an amusing purpose is also a useful one. More utility than this, however, can be claimed for the wood of the Elder. Its young wood is said to be especially sweet and wholesome, and is consequently more fit than other wood employed for the purpose for use as skewers for meat and for the flesh of fowls and game. It is further used by shoemakers for pegging boots, is valued by turners because it will take a good polish, and is not, when mature, unlike Box in colour, and may therefore be made into many fancy articles for use and adornment. In ancient times it is said that the hollow tubes formed by the branches when their abnormally large-columns of pith were extracted, were manufactured into musical instruments, and in proof of this assertion the generic botanical name is instanced, *Sambuca* indicating a musical instrument. *Sambuca* really means a species of harp, but not impossibly the meaning might have been made elastic to suit the use to which those tubes were put. *Sambuca* also means a machine for storming fortifications. The prophet Joshua and his followers blew down the walls of Jericho and stormed that city by means of blasts sounded seven times upon rams' horns. Twisted Elder tubes might have made almost as loud sounds as the rams' horns, and *Sambucus* means the Elder-tree. The pith of the Elder is used in electrical experiments, and the wood not only makes excellent charcoal for gunpowder, but, when it has acquired age, it is as hard nearly as Box.

The wood of the Common Elm (*Ulmus campestris*) has long had a great reputation for hardness and durability. It has a fine grain, and is used very much for the woodwork of ships because it is especially adapted to bear exposure to alternate sun, rain, and water, without either warping or cracking or splitting. For the receptacles of frail humanity, for casks, for boxes required for their strength, for that part of the woodwork of buildings, of bridges, of quays, and of other constructions exposed constantly to the action of water, its peculiar qualities of hardness, solidity, and durability render it invaluable.

Dark in colour, close-grained in texture, hard and heavy, capable of a fine polish, and durable and flexible, the wood of the Evergreen Oak or Ilex (*Quercus ilex*) is naturally valuable. For mallet-heads, beetles, axle-trees, wedges (when great hardness is required), wooden pins, palisades, and for the woodwork used about fortifications, as well as for the stocks of tools, it is excellently fitted, and is much employed. It also makes excellent charcoal.

The Guelder Rose (*Viburnum opulus*) does not claim a long catalogue of uses, but its wood, being hard, is made into skewers and put to some of the offices of the Dogwood.

Perhaps the most frequent use of the Hawthorn

(*Cratægus oxyacantha*) is for walking-sticks. Its toughness, hardness, and durability, and its capability of receiving a high polish render it peculiarly valuable for this purpose. Its wood is not commonly found growing at a large size, and, hence, it is made useful in small ways, as, for instance, for the handles of hammers and mallets, and for flails, as well as for the teeth of mill-wheels, where timber, and not iron, is still employed. Though it has some of the qualities of Box, being of a yellowish tinge, fine in grain, hard and susceptible of a high polish, it is not likely to be a substitute for the engraving-wood on account of its liability to warp; and the difficulty of working it prevents it from being largely used by the turner, joiner, and cabinet-maker.

In times gone by sticks of the Hazel (*Corylus avellana*) were used as divining-rods for discovering the presence of minerals in the earth. Perhaps, for an equally good reason, they may have been employed to make the charcoal of the alchemists. In any case, the wood does make excellent charcoal. It is much employed, however, for fishing-rods, on account of its durability

THORN AND IVY.

and elasticity, for walking-sticks—for that purpose the bark is very commonly left on as an
ornament—for hoops, and for rustic work, garden
chairs, tables, &c.

Hickory wood, though coarse-grained, is very
strong, heavy, and durable, and is useful for
innumerable purposes for which these timber
qualities are essential. It is also elastic, and
is employed frequently for the manufacture of
carriages.

Whiteness of colour, hardness of grain, and a
high susceptibility of polish are qualities which
commend the Holly (*Ilex aquifolium*) as a most
valuable tree, and especially for the production of
articles for ornament. It is even said to have
been employed at times as a substitute for Box in
wood-engraving. Its hardness, too, has suggested
the feasibility of employing it as a substitute for
ebony and for other woods, dyes of various hues
being employed to disguise it. For the making
of mathematical instruments, for cabinet-work,
and for the purposes of the joiner it is admirably
adapted, although, from the fact of its not
ordinarily growing to a large size, except in

remote forests, its wood is not obtainable in large quantity. So fine, hard, and compact is its grain, and so white is its substance, that portions, highly polished, have been likened to ivory.

Another hard and close-grained wood, that of the Hornbeam (*Carpinus betulus*), though possessing great strength and durability, will not take a good polish, and hence is not so useful for many purposes on that account. It is heavy, and possesses great strength. It makes, too, capital charcoal, and produces, in burning, great heat. In its comparatively young state the wood of the Hornbeam is used for many kinds of wheelwright's work, for mill-cogs, and other purposes where toughness and hardness are requisite.

The Horse Chestnut (*Æsculus hippocastanum*) possesses qualities which are the reverse of the woods last mentioned, for mainly, no doubt on account of its rapidity of growth, its wood is soft, not very strong, and not very durable where much exposure to the weather is requisite; but it is sometimes used for plank-flooring, cart-linings, and packing-cases, and for purposes where hardness, toughness, fineness of grain, and the quality of durability are not needed. Judging by the stalwart appearance of this tree when growing, and by its apparent robustness of constitution, one would imagine that it might rival in utility many of the woods of commerce; but such, in reality, is not the case.

Density of fibre is the quality that usually determines the value of wood; the denser the fibre, the harder and heavier the timber, and the greater its commercial importance, because this density of substance means durability. But this particular quality of wood is acquired by slow growth, and the quantity produced being thus naturally limited—because the crops take so long to mature—the material, as a commercial product, becomes consequently more costly. Within the category of such slow-growing, heavy woods comes one of the most remarkable of them all, the Ironwood, which is so heavy that it sinks in water, a given quantity of this wood being much heavier than its equal bulk of water. The Ironwood tree is related to the Hornbeams, and

not distantly related to the Oak. Here is a
group of these hard woods' which includes the
species just indicated—the natural order *Cupu-
liferæ* comprising about 400 species, and compre-
hending three tribes. Of these, *Betuleæ* include
the Birches and the Alders; *Coryleæ* the Hazels,
the Hornbeams, and the Ironwoods; and *Quercineæ*
the Oaks, Beeches, and Chestnuts. There are two
species of Ironwood, one belonging to the genus
Ostrya and one to *Olneya*. The most valuable of
the former, having regard to the quality of its
wood, is *Ostrya virginica*, the other is *Olneya
tesota*.

It will hardly be expected that the Ivy (*Hedera
helix*) could produce any wood of service, and it
is an exception to find this climbing tree of
sufficient size to contain a timber stem; yet there
is a use made of its wood when of sufficient size—
that may be new to many people. It is not hard,
though slow-growing, and it is, moreover, porous.
It is therefore used by being cut into thin slices
for filtering liquids. The wood of large roots is
also sometimes made into 'strops' for sharpen-
ing knives.

A very beautiful wood is that produced by the Judas tree (*Cercis siliquastrum*). It is prettily spotted or blotched on a ground of grey, with wavy marks of green, yellow, and black ; and, as it will take a high polish, it is valuable for the manufacture of numerous fancy articles.

The Junipers, of which the Common Juniper (*Juniperus communis*) is a representative species, are handsome trees, though generally so small-growing as not to produce wood in any considerable quantity or of any considerable size ; but what is obtained is valuable. The colour of the wood of *Juniperus communis* is yellowish-brown, but it is finely veined, very durable, will take a high polish, and is, moreover, aromatic. Another species of the genus, called the Red Cedar (*Juniperus virginiana*), produces coloured wood, largely used for the manufacture of the wooden envelopes of black-lead pencils. In this tree the heart-wood is of a beautiful red colour, whilst, curiously enough, the sap-wood is quite white.

Another wood that is frequently used to imitate Ebony is that of the Laburnum. In some species of the genus *Cytisus* the wood is greenish-black, and being hard and durable, and capable of taking a high polish, it is much used. for the manufacture of fancy boxes and other articles. The heart-wood in all the trees of this genus is dark, and it is darker in the Common Laburnum (*Cytisus laburnum*) than in some of the others. Turners and cabinet-makers therefore put it to good use. It is used also for the staves of casks, and for making noggins or wooden mugs or cups. Punch-ladles are also made from this wood, and it is sometimes employed in the manufacture of musical instruments, and in former times it was used in the making of bows.

Lancewood is familiar to everybody from its use for bows and fishing-rods. In the south of Africa the natives make the stems of their spears of this wood, and its use for lance-making has, of course, originated its name. The tree which produces it is the Lancewood tree (*Guatteria virgata*) and is a native of Jamaica. Though not a large-growing tree, its wood is very valuable for its peculiar qualities of elasticity and tough-ness. This wood is not only elastic, but strong, and of close and uniform grain. For other purposes, when these qualities are desirable, such as for making light shafts of carriages, the wood is in request. Another species of Lancewood is produced by the Hassagay tree (*Curtisia faginea*). This tree grows to a larger size than the one just mentioned, and yields very valuable timber, which is applied to purposes very similar to those of *Guatteria virgata*.

The uses of the Larch (*Larix europæa*) are almost innumerable. Its wood has been said to be the most useful of any of the species of the useful genus *Abies* which includes the Firs. In colour it is of a reddish-brown, and for all purposes of domestic architecture it is invaluable—for floors, for windows, for beams and joists and doors; and for all sorts of open uses in which there is exposure to the weather, its enduring qualities are pre-eminently serviceable. Absence of knots in its timber is one very valuable quality which takes it out of the category of common deals. Its good colour, toughness and hardness; its susceptibility of a high polish, its damp-resisting character, and its almost fire-resisting quality give it recommendation of the first importance. For use in the ship-building trades, and for employment in making railway sleepers and for other railway purposes, where exposure to the weather is involved, it is unrivalled. The outdoor uses for wood are almost numberless, and Larch is second to none in all the necessary qualifications of timber for such uses.

Famous amongst heavy woods is the *Lignum vitæ* or 'wood of life,' the botanical name of which is *Guaiacum officinale*. It is an evergreen, with dark foliage, and grows in its native country, the West Indian islands, to a large size. The wood is yellow, or a yellow inclining to olive colour, with an irregular cross grain. It is so hard that it is extremely difficult to split it, and it breaks, when struck heavily, almost in the manner of stone. The resinous sap it contains resists the entrance into its substance of water, and this circumstance explains its remarkable resistance to decay. Its heaviest and hardest and also its darkest-coloured part is its heart-wood—its sap-wood being less heavy and of a lighter colour. For all uses in which exceptional hardness is required—such as for mallets and stamps, for block-pulleys, and for employments where wood, though used in preference to metal, nevertheless requires to possess almost the hardness of metal, *Lignum vitæ* is desiderated.

Amenability to the knife causes the wood of the Lime tree, of which the best known is the Common Lime (*Tilia europæa*), to be much esteemed by carvers and gilders; for, soft in character, though in quality close-grained, light, and smooth, and in colour pale yellow or almost white, it is a capital wood for cutting into any desired form. Hence for toys, games, and all sorts of manufactured things which require to be cut into particular shapes, this wood is admirably adapted. For the sounding-boards of pianos, for boards for shoemakers and glovers for cutting their work out upon, for making mouldings and designs in wood, it is an excellent material. Indeed, the Lime was called ' the carvers' tree,' and it is said that Grinling Gibbons preferred it to any other wood for his carvings.

The wonderful and beautiful Mahogany demands some notice, though its uses are too well known to need enumeration. The botanical name of the principal tree which produces it is *Swietenia mahoganii*, a truly majestic tree, which is believed to require two hundred years of growth to produce perfect timber—the slow growth being, as in the case of other trees, the secret of its elaborate perfection.

Of Maples there are many, but let us take a typical species by selecting the Common or Field Maple (*Acer campestre*), whose wood is very handsome, fine-grained, compact, often beautifully veined, and susceptible of a high polish. The woody roots of this tree are not unfrequently elegantly knotted, and then possess especial value, being made into pipes, snuff-boxes, and various articles of taste or luxury. In olden times it was held in great estimation. Gilpin, referring to this circumstance, says : ' Pliny * speaks as highly of the knobs and excrescences of this tree, called the *brusca* and *mollusca*, as Dr. Plot does of those of the Ash.† The veins of these excrescences in the Maple, Pliny tells us, were so variegated that they exceeded the beauty

* See Plin. Nat. Hist. lib. xvi. ch. 16.
† Met. lib. x. v. 2.

of any other wood, even of the Citron ; though the Citron was in such repute at Rome that Cicero, who was neither rich nor expensive, was tempted to give ten thousand sesterces for a Citron table. The brusca and mollusca, Pliny adds, were rarely of size sufficient for the larger species of furniture ; but in all smaller cabinet-work they were inestimable. Indeed, the whole tree was esteemed by the ancients, on account of its variegated wood. In Ovid we find it thus celebrated :

"Acerque coloribus impar." *

How far, at this day, it may be valued for cabinet-work, I know not. I have, here and there, seen boxes and other little things made of it, which I have thought beautiful. But I am told that in North America, where it grows wild, it is in much esteem. When the cabinet-maker meets with a knotted tree of this kind, which is there called the *curled Maple*, he prizes it highly.' †

The Mulberry (*Morus*) should, from the interest which surrounds it as a silkworm-feeder and a

* Met. lib. x. v. 1.—The maple stained with various hues.
† 'Forest Scenery,' pages 81-2.

fruit-producer, deserve some reference to its timber; for though it is not accounted of great value amongst timber-trees, its wood does possess qualities of strength, closeness of grain, and durability. As to the last-mentioned quality, it is said that it will remain sound when immersed in water as long as the best Oak.

Who can recount the virtues, and describe the qualities of Oak? Its reputation is too universal, its utility too commonly understood to need re-stating. Its slow growth is doubtless the secret of its great value for solidity, compactness, hardness, toughness, and durability. For use in ship-building, in house-building, in the manufacture of furniture, in the construction of every kind of woodwork requiring the finest qualities of strength, beauty, and endurance, it is indeed unrivalled. Not merely, as we intimate, for its marvellous character for strength of fibre and durability is it entitled to fame. No wood is more susceptible of a beautiful polish, and scarcely any furniture is more esteemed, both for elegance and utility, than that made of Oak. Almost everything could be said in favour of its wonderful qualities, without exhausting its praises; but we have said enough, perhaps, to indicate that this noble tree is really beyond praise. Gilpin has some very happy remarks on this subject. Prefacing them by observing that 'amongst deciduous trees, the Oak presents itself first' for consideration, he goes on to say that ' it is a happiness to the lovers of the picturesque, that this noble plant is as useful as it is beautiful. From the utility of the Oak, they derive this advantage, that it is everywhere found. In the choice indeed of its soil it is rather delicate. For though it is rather undistinguishing during its early growth, while its horizontal fibres straggle about the surface of the earth; yet when its tap-root begins to enter the depths of the soil, perhaps no tree is nicer in its discriminations. If its constitution be not suited here, it may multiply its progeny indeed, and produce a thriving copse; but the puny race will never rise to lordly dignity in the forest, nor furnish navies to command the ocean.'

Gilpin adds a note at this point: ' How quickly the Oak vegetates in a soil it likes, may be seen from the following instance :—" An acorn was sown at Beckett, the seat of Lord Barrington, on the day of his birth in 1717. In November, 1790, it contained ninety-five feet of timber, which at 2*s.* per foot would sell for 9*l.* 10*s.* The top was valued at about 1*l.* 15*s.* The girth, at five feet from the ground, was about half an inch more than eight feet. The increase of girth in the two last years was $4\frac{1}{2}$ inches. It grows in rich land, worth 1*l.* 5*s.* an acre." '*

Referring to the qualities of its timber, Gilpin proceeds : ' The particular, and most valued qualities of the Oak are *hardness* and *toughness.* Shakespeare uses two epithets to express these qualities, which are perhaps stronger than any we can find.

> " Thou rather with thy sharp and sulph'rous bolt
> Split'st the *unwedgeable* and *gnarled* Oak,
> Than the soft Myrtle."

' Many kinds of wood are *harder*, as Box and Ebony ; many kinds are *tougher*, as Yew and Ash ; but it is supposed that no species of wood,

* ' Forest Scenery,' pages 41-2.

at least no species of timber, is possessed of both these qualities together in so great a degree as British Oak. Almost all arts and manufactures are indebted to it; but in ship-building, and bearing burdens, its elasticity and strength are applied to most advantage. I mention these *mechanic uses* only because some of its *chief beauties* are connected with them. Thus it is not the erect, stately tree that is always the most useful in ship-building; but more often the crooked one, forming short turns, and elbows, which the shipwrights and carpenters commonly call *knee-timber*. This too is generally the most picturesque. Nor is it the straight, tall stem, whose fibres run in parallel lines, that is the most useful in bearing burdens: but that whose sinews are twisted and spirally combined. This too is the most picturesque. Trees under these circumstances generally take the most pleasing forms. Now the Oak, perhaps, acquires these different modes of growth from the different strata through which it passes. In deep, rich soils, where the root meets no obstruction, the stem, we suppose, grows stately and erect: but when the root meets

with a rocky stratum, a hard and gravelly bed, or
any other difficulty, through which it is obliged,
in a zigzag course, to pick its way, and struggle
for a passage, the sympathetic stem, feeling every
motion, pursues the same indirect course above,
which the root does below : and thus the sturdy
plant, through the means of these subterraneous
encounters and hardy conflicts, assumes form
and character, and becomes, in a due course of
centuries, a picturesque tree.'*

Even a thousand years after cutting from the
tree affords no criterion of the marvellous durability of Oak. After nearly double that period
the wood retains its marvellous freshness, and
seems indeed to be almost imperishable. When
workmen were engaged in clearing the channel at
Brundusium in Italy, they came upon Oak piles
which were driven into the bed of the channel
by Julius Cæsar, to block up Pompey's fleet ; they
were the whole trunks of young Oaks, from
which the bark had been stripped, and though
they had been immersed under seven feet of sand
for more than eighteen hundred years, it is stated

* 'Forest Scenery,' pages 43-4.

SCOTCH FIR.   YEW.

that they were as fresh as if they had only been cut from the woods a few weeks before. Marvellous, indeed, are these facts.

We could go on voluminously to record facts corroborative of the wonderful quality and endurance of Oak, instancing attested cases in which the doors of public buildings, made ten, twelve, and even fifteen hundred years ago, were still almost as good as when made; but our allotted space will not allow of the continuation of this subject, interesting though it be, for the claims of other trees to discussion must be considered.

A tree whose wood admits more readily than that of many other trees of being stained black in imitation of Ebony, is the well-known and fruitful Pear (*Pyrus communis*, ' common ' indeed, but beautiful). Naturally the colour of Pear wood is slightly reddish. It is finely and closely grained, strong and heavy. In past times it was considered of value for wood-engravings, but never had the same estimation as the inimitable Box, being used only for the coarser designs. For other purposes also it is employed by the turner and the

joiner, apart from the use made of it in its dis-
guised form—its form when 'ebonized.'

To give a discriminating account of the wood
of the useful Pine would require a considerable
amount of space. We must therefore be content
to limit our remarks to one very typical tree—
the Scotch Pine (*Pinus sylvestris*), which includes
within itself nearly all the properties, and nearly
all the virtues of the race of Pines. How much
human habitations in all parts of the world owe,
for the material of which they are constructed,
to the 'deal' furnished by the wonderfully
useful Pines, only timber statisticians could even
approximately state. The white, coloured, or
yellow and resinous wood produced from these
prolific and singularly valuable trees has been
distributed in countless quantities all over the
universe. The proof of the remarkable sound-
ness and durability of the timber of the Scotch
Pine is found in the fact that after doing service
in the roofs of houses for centuries, it is found to
be perfectly good and in a remarkable state of
preservation. Combined with its strength, durability, and freedom from knots, it is remarkable

for its lightness and quality—a double characteristic, very often of especial importance in wood.
In colour Scotch Pine-wood is reddish, but the
colours of the timber of the other species of the
genus *Pinus* and of the allied genus *Abies* (the Firs)
varies much, inclining from what is called white to
various shades of yellow ; and varying, as we have
said, in quality and in its greater or less freedom
from knots ; but all possess the great qualification
of wide utility, for no other kind of timber has anything like the same universal application to all the
purposes of domestic, commercial, and naval architecture.

The wood of the elegant and picturesque Plane,
of which there are two species, *Platanus orientalis*
and *Platanus occidentalis*, is not highly valued,
but, like the tree itself, it may be said to be
' picturesque.' In some parts of the world it is
still used by the carpenter, the cabinet-maker,
and the joiner—for the timber, though naturally
yellow or yellowish-white, as the tree attains age,
becomes brown, the ground of that colour being
marked with elegant veins or markings like
jasper. If rubbed with oil, it will take a high

polish, and can then be made into ornamental articles resembling somewhat the wood of the Walnut-tree.

Hard in texture, the wood of the Wild Plum (*Prunus spinosa*) takes a fine polish, but is not of much use, owing to its liability to crack. It is, however, employed in some cases for making the handles of tools, and, on account of its hardness, for the teeth of various agricultural implements, such as wooden rakes. For walking-sticks, however, the Blackthorn is largely employed, on account of the same quality of hardness, and also on account of its beauty—for Wild Plum walking-sticks are, it is well known, very handsome.

Another wood not commonly much esteemed is that of the Poplar (*Populus*). The same general lack of estimation extends to the various species of this genus. The rapidity of growth of the Poplars causes the wood to be light and soft, and that prevents it from acquiring that closeness of grain and compactness so essential to good timber. In colour, most of these woods are light, inclining to yellow. For toy-making

they are serviceable; also for some kinds of
cabinet-making. Its employment in buildings,
for floors, is sometimes suggested because of its
whiteness, the readiness with which it can be
cleaned, and the difficulty with which it can be
ignited. The White Poplar (*Populus alba*), the
Black Poplar (*Populus nigra*), the Lombardy
Poplar (*Populus fastigiata*), the Aspen or Trem-
bling Poplar (*Populus tremula*), and the Grey
Poplar (*Populus canescens*) are the best known of
these trees. The whitest woods are those of the
White and the Grey Poplars, that of the latter
being the harder of the two. They are used for
packing-cases, for drapers' bobbins and rollers,
for toys, and for some of the inferior purposes
of the cabinet-maker and turner. The wood of
the Aspen, being exceptionally light, is used for
inferior casks, such as casks for packing fish, for
milk-pails, for clogs, sabots, butchers' trays, and
sometimes by sculptors and engravers for inferior
work. The Black Poplar is so called, according
to one explanation, because of a black circle found
within the centre of its trunk. In the wood produced by some individuals of this species there

are mottled knots, and, when polished, this wood makes handsome and ornamental boxes.

Useful in a humble degree is the Spindle Tree (*Euonymus europæus*), whose close-grained, hard wood is employed in making spindles and skewers. Formerly it was used by musical instrument makers, and in the present day it furnishes, when reduced to charcoal, a capital drawing material for artists.

As the Scotch Pine amongst Pines claims superiority for its timber, so may the Spruce Fir (*Abies excelsa*) be said to deserve pre-eminence amongst the Firs. Its wood is both elastic and light, it is durable, sometimes red and sometimes yellowish in colour—durability and colour depending a good deal on the soil in which it grows—and it is extremely resinous. Potash is produced by its ashes. For the masts of vessels, for which whole trees, stripped of their bark, are used; for ladders, scaffold and other poles; for oars of boats, and for other aquatic purposes; for the flooring of houses, sometimes for making musical instruments; for packing-boxes, for the interiors of cabinets and drawers, and occasionally for carvers and gilders it is used. It is capable of taking a high polish, and is amenable to the arts of the stainer and 'ebonizer.'

Sycamore wood, by which we mean the wood of the Great Maple (*Acer pseudo-platanus*), though finely grained, capable of polishing, and sometimes veined, is used for various purposes of no great importance. It can be easily worked, and hence joiners and cabinet-makers put it to a useful employment. Wooden spoons and other domestic utensils used to be made of this material, and gunstocks, cider-presses, and musical instruments are still made of it. It is not very hard, and its colour, white at first, becomes, as the tree matures, yellowish and sometimes brown. One very useful property it has is its non-liability to warp; and a proof of its durability, notwithstanding its comparative softness, is the fact that the wooden envelopes or coffins in which mummies were placed in the Eastern catacombs were invariably made of Sycamore wood. Lastly, it makes excellent fuel, and, when burning, gives out a great deal of heat.

The True Service Tree (*Pyrus sorbus*) is said

by Loudon to be ' the hardest and the heaviest of
all the indigenous woods of Europe.'   He adds :
' It weighs, when dry, no less than seventy-two
pounds two ounces per cubic foot.   It has a compact fine grain, a reddish tinge, and takes a very
high   polish; but it must not be employed
until it is thoroughly seasoned, as otherwise
it is apt to twist and split.   It is much
sought after in France by mill-wrights for making
cogs to wheels, rollers, cylinders, blocks and
pulleys, spindles and axles, and for all those
parts of machines which are subject to much
friction and require great strength and durability.
In France it is preferred to all other kinds of
wood for making the screws to wine-presses.

Very close in texture, hard, and heavy is the
wood of the Whitebeam (*Pyrus aria*).   It is
yellow or yellowish-white in colour, and will take a
high polish.   Handles to various articles are made
from it, and it can easily be stained to imitate
other woods when desired.   It used to be, and
still is to a considerable extent, employed for
cogs to wheels of machinery.

Of the Willow (*Salix*) the uses are pretty well

known. The manufacture of baskets from the twigs is one of the most extensive uses to which this tree is put, the wood being very light as well as soft and smooth. Cricket-bails, bats, fish-coracles, and many other things of less importance are manufactured from it.

Last to consider in this examination of woods is the Yew (*Taxus baccata*). Its extreme slowness of growth promotes the compactness, hardness, closeness of grain, flexibility, elasticity, and, it may finally be said, the incorruptibility of its timber. Besides all these fine qualities, Yew wood is a beautiful colour, orange-red inclining to deep brown. Where the sap-wood and the heart-wood join in the trunk, there are varying shades of colour—brown, red, and white. These, joined to the waviness of the grain, give a very beautiful appearance. The term waviness in this case is very well applied, for the resemblance of the figures made in the wood is like the waters of a sea, not only when in motion, but when troubled. When polished—and the wood of the Yew is susceptible of a very high polish—the appearance just indicated is very beautiful. If when veneer has been cut from a Yew log, the veneer be steeped for a few months in the waters of a pond, it will, it is stated by Varennes de Feuilles, 'take a purple-violet colour.' This, however, is not always the case, at least with the solid logs of the wood, after immersion in water. We have before us a specimen—forwarded to us from Ireland by Mr. Archibald Henderson, of Clonad, Tullamore—of Yew wood. It was taken from the trunk of a tree dug out of the Killenmore bog, King's County, in June, 1883. It is impossible to say how long this trunk had lain in the bog, but probably for hundreds of years; yet it is as light in colour, and as fresh in appearance as if just cut from a newly-felled tree, and it possesses in a remarkable degree the waviness to which we have referred. Not only does Yew wood mature so slowly, but, after cutting, it takes longer to dry than any other known wood. Compensation, however, for this circumstance is found in the fact that it loses very little indeed in the process of drying, not more than one forty-eighth part of its bulk. A cubic foot, when dry, weighs sixty-one pounds and seven ounces. The fineness of the grain of Yew wood is very remarkable, and as au illustration of this fact, it may be stated that in 280 years the tree only adds twenty inches to its diameter, for 280 annual concentric rings have been counted within a diameter of twenty inches. This statement must, of course, be taken as an average one ; for with the Yew, as with other trees, cold and ungenial, and warm and 'growing' seasons make some difference, though probably not any appreciable difference in most cases, for the 'cycles' of weather would be pretty nearly equalized in a space of 280 years. It will be easily understood that Yew timber makes one of the finest woods for the purposes of the cabinet-maker. In olden times, it is well known, it was employed in the making of bows, and amongst its pre-eminently valuable qualifications in the present day is not only its adaptibility for manufacturing into the finest descriptions of furniture and frame-work, but for employment in all out door service requiring exceptional durability. One remarkable proof of the estimation in which the Yew is held in the English New Forest is a saying of the inhabitants that ' a post of Yew will outlast a post of iron.'

III.

H OW wonderful and beautiful is the arrangement by which plants obtain the rest that with them, as with all beings and things that *grow*, is essential to their well-being in the wise economy of Nature !
We do not here allude to the really curious and interesting arrangements by which leaves during the night in Summer alter their position, and, so to speak, fold themselves up to sleep. Familiar examples of this singular function are afforded in the case of the pretty Wood Sorrel (*Oxalis acetosella*), which folds its upper surfaces, that most require protection, together during the night, and unfolds them again in the morning;

in the case of the common Clover (*Trifolium repens*), and in that of some other plants. Many flowers, too, as is well known, close their petals during the darkness as if for rest, and open them again on the appearance of sunlight. But our allusion is to the Winter sleep of plants and seeds, and marvellous and interesting indeed are the innumerable provisions made for promoting, maintaining, and protecting this sleep. The heralding, or rather the signalling of the Winter night-time—if the expression may be used—is the fall of the leaf. Then follows, in deciduous trees, the falling of the sap and that quiescent state which indicates the period of rest. Roots, stem, and branches all cease their active functions. Evergreens, it is true, preserve their verdancy; but there is no upward motion or progress. In their case, as in that of deciduous plants, the progression of vital forces is arrested; but elaborate preparation has already been made for the green and floral display of the succeeding seasons, and elaborate protection has been afforded for the organs which will be exposed to the wintry cold. Summer and autumn, sun and wind, have ripened the branches that have been developed from the ·buds in the earlier months. Their bark, first green and tender, has become embrowned and hardened, thus producing warmth and protection for the soft and tender tissue in them, and preserving the delicacy and perfection of the moist channels that convey the plant's life-blood—the sap—first down into the trunk and roots, where it can receive protection during the period of rest, and then up again to create life and beauty when the succeeding spring dawns upon the woods. The effect of frost upon these delicate vessels would be ruinous to their vitality and vigour. But everything has been anticipated. The leaves, which are thin, tender, and delicate, as are those of deciduous plants, fall away and leave the rough and well-prepared branches which bore them to withstand the wintry cold. The leaves of evergreens which remain during the season of sleep, are prepared by long exposure and by the hardening and thickening of their epidermis, or outer coating of cellular tissue, to withstand the severest influences of Winter.

IV.

MBRYOS of future plants are protected by the most elaborate and beautiful arrangements from all ungenial influences by hard and horny *outer* coverings, varnished and thickly gummed to exclude both cold and moisture, and by the softest of silky wraps *within*. The marvellous variety of the provisions for the protection of the seed is so great that a large volume could be filled with the interesting details; but let us take an instance that will illustrate the wise and beautiful economy of the world—one of the commonest that dwellers in towns, as well as

residents in the country, can see for themselves
with little trouble, if they wish to minutely study
the ways of kind Nature in this department of her
great laboratory. Few dormant seeds, perhaps,
are there that look less interesting and less
attractive, and more brown and dead, than the
pods which depend plentifully from the twigs of the
Common Laburnum. Let us take one down from
the tree in mid-Winter, and look at it. The pod
is dark brown and dead-looking, and the marks
on the outside indicate the position of the seeds
within. It is a pretty sight that is disclosed
when it is opened, splitting as it does into two
parts longitudinally ; for a beautiful provision is
made within for protecting the seeds from the
wintry cold. The pod is two inches long, and
contains six purple-black and somewhat kidney-
shaped seeds attached by their indented sides to
the side of the pod, three seeds each side, arranged
alternately, so that when the pod is closed, they
are in a line, and economy of space is strictly
observed. The pod is lined in each trough or
half with a very pale yellow, silky lining, which
separates from the hard and shiny substance of

STONE PINE.

LARCH.

the pod itself. Upon this soft couch the seeds obtain warmth and protection from the cold. The seeds themselves are protected by water-proof coverings, capable of affording a certain amount of protection from the cold ; and should they prematurely fall by the too easy splitting of their silk-lined, horny envelope, there is still the chance of their falling to the ground and lying between substances which would render them cold-proof.

How marvellously diverse indeed are the provisions made for protecting the delicate germ which encloses the wonderful principle of vitality called life ! In the Chestnut and Walnut there is first the thick and prickly outer shell of green tissue, then within that—in the case of the Walnut—there is a stout hard shell, then a close covering of brown skin, then the albuminous matter which immediately surrounds the actual plant-germ or embryo. In the case of the Chestnut, there is first—within the prickly outer shell—an inner glossy one like polished mahogany, and inside that the brown skin enclosing the mass of albumen.

In the plum there is, inside the sweet, fleshy

pulp, the hard shelly substance called the stone, and inside that the kernel, itself enwrapped in brown skin. In the apple, pear, strawberry, gooseberry, orange, and other soft-bodied fruits, a mass of sweet, soft substance encloses the more or less hard or horny covering of the seed-germs.

Endless are the shades of colour, and endless are the markings of seeds—red, black, purple, green—spotted, splashed, and veined; and within, the seed sleeps until the awakening forces of warmth and moisture in the succeeding spring set in motion the complex and exquisitely beautiful machinery which, with subtle mystery, fashions stem and radicle, leaves, flowers, and fruit.

How perfect is the protection afforded to the beautiful life within the seed-envelope is scarcely apprehended by those who regard a dormant seed as merely a tiny, dingy-coloured, and insignificant thing. Nature adapts her processes to suit her particular needs, and hence it is that the coverings she fashions are so various. The seeds which, like those of the Pines, are produced by trees which grow in the roughest and wildest parts of

the earth, where storms and winds exercise their
most powerful effects, and where great hardness
and vitality are essential to preservation, are
especially protected by complex arrangements from
injury and from premature dampness. The Pine-
cone—hard, woody, and rain-proof—is a wonderful envelope for the seed—an envelope of singular
strength and endurance, and one capable of preserving the vitality of the Pine-germs for marvellously long periods of time. Convulsions of the
world's surface, though sometimes involving a
sacrifice of human life, have all some wise purpose,
and are always followed by compensatory influences. When by any convulsion of Nature the
surface of the ground is dismantled and stripped
temporarily of its vegetable growth, provision is
duly made for the reappearance of that green life
which is the earth's essential garment. But for
the vitality of seeds which are temporarily buried,
and apparently destroyed by such violent changes,
there might be no sufficient succession of fertility.
It is the fact, however—of which undoubted proof
exists—that seeds buried in geologic strata that
have remained buried under overlying seams of

earth, sand, or rock, have, when brought to the surface and subjected to the influence of sun and rain, developed into life!

Many years ago in North America, whilst some men were engaged in the operation of digging a well, they came upon a stratum of sea-sand at some distance from the surface. Its discovery gave rise to much curiosity, as there was no sea near the place. The sand therefore was carefully collected and thrown down by itself for further examination. Some time afterwards plants were discovered growing from the sand, and on being identified, it was found they were specimens of *Prunus maritima*—' the seaside inhabiting Plum,' as it is called—a species which only grows wild by the sea-shore. The plum-stones enclosing the fertile kernel had probably lain for many centuries in the position in which they were found, and had passed through geologic changes of considerable violence without injury! Dr. Lindley, famous for his works on botany, stated that he had raised three raspberry plants from seeds which had been taken from a human skeleton dug up from a Roman barrow, the skeleton being thirty feet under the ground! It is even averred that some withered kidney-beans, obtained from a bag that was taken from the window-seat of one of the houses dug out from the ruins of Herculaneum, came up when planted, and blossomed! Sleep only though this be, it is, indeed, sleep profound.

V.

UDGED by outward appearance, it would be utterly impossible to form even an approximate estimate of the ages of trees. Yet the results which have been published of inquiries in this most interesting direction have led to satisfactory conclusions; but the data have been obtained in various ways, and by a process of deduction, rather than by actual and direct evidence. The deductions have, nevertheless, been so clear as to leave little room for doubt, and for the reason that when they have been put to the test against clearly ascertained facts, they have proved to be sound.

In the case of all exogenous trees—those whose additions of cellular matter are made in concentric rings externally to their substance— the scientific test of age is the number of such concentric rings shown in the trunk, as each cylinder of matter annually formed can be distinguished from the preceding or succeeding cylinders in all cases except those of the first and last. When the outer cylinders of its wood are capable of being counted—by not being broken and confused—the age of the tree corresponds in years with the number of rings shown on a cross section, or a cutting through the trunk in a direction horizontal to the ground. But this process could only be tried by the destruction of the tree, and if that process only of finding out had to be applied, no criterion could be formed of the ages of living trees. But historical notes and coincident events have thrown some light on the subject, and experts have, by a knowledge of the whole subject, been able to arrive at some satisfactory results; so that it may be assumed that the data now to be given are based on a solid foundation, though they are of course only approximate. Taking the trees in the order of their longevity, the list will be headed by the Yew with 3200 years. Then comes the Cedar with 3000, an estimate which is partly based upon the assumption that the existing Cedars of Lebanon were contemporaries of Solomon. The approximate ages of the others about which information has been obtained are : Wellingtonia, 2000 ; Oak, 1650 ; Plane, 1300 ; Spruce, 1200 ; Lime, 1100 ; Chestnut, 1000 ; Sycamore, 1000 ; Walnut, 900 ; Cypress, 800 ; Beech, 800 ; Olive, 800 ; Orange, 630 ; Elm, 600 ; Larch, 576 ; Maple, 516 ; Ivy, 335 ; Ash, 300, Barberry, 300 ; Scotch Fir, 250 ; White Poplar, 160 ; Thorn, 150 ; Vine, 100 ; and Mountain Ash, 100. It must be distinctly understood that whilst these ages have been supplied upon the best authority obtainable, it is not to be assumed that the periods indicated may not be inconsistent with some actually ascertained facts. The reason for this is that circumstances of growth occasion the most important differences in the duration of tree-life. Trees growing under apparently the most favourable conditions often, for unexplained and frequently incomprehensible reasons, decay and die at a comparatively early age; and in other cases individuals, not more favourably situated to all appearance than others, live to an abnormally great age, far beyond the average of the species. Although, for instance, the age of the Wellingtonia has been given here at 2000 years, the following remarkable statement will point to a probably much longer duration of life. It will take the form of an extract from a communication made to the *Gardeners' Chronicle* by Sir J. D. Hooker. Speaking of a specimen of Wellingtonia felled in 1875, the writer stated that the girth *inside* the bark at four feet from the ground was 107 feet! He continued: 'Its wood was very compact, and showed, throughout a considerable portion of the trunk, thirty annual rings to the inch. This, if the rings were of uniform diameter in the rest of the trunk, would give the incredible age of 6400; but as the interior rings of such trees are much broader than the outer, half that number to the inch is a more conceivable estimate, and would give an average of 3500 years! The only other instance of careful counting which we can find is that of the felled tree in the Calaveras Grove, which measured seventy feet in girth inside the bark at six feet above the ground, and which at forty feet above the ground had 1255 rings. In this case the rings next the bark were thirty-three to the inch—a number which at five feet inward had diminished one-half.' Sir Joseph Hooker chiefly obtained his information, he stated, from some accurate data supplied by Mr. Muir.

Mr. Wilfrid George Marshall, in his interesting book, 'Through America,' records an instance of the counting of rings in a prostrate trunk of *Wellingtonia gigantea* in the Calaveras Grove in California. The reference is so important that we will quote entire the paragraph containing it. Mr. Marshall says, 'Now, concerning the age of these giant *Wellingtonias*, it seems hard to comprehend their antiquity, even with such facts before one as are to be found in the immense number of rings that can be counted on some of the severed prostrate trunks. My friend' (a travelling companion) 'counted in one tree as many as two thousand rings. If each one of these rings represents a year's growth, then this tree is two thousand years old at the very least. Report goes that a tree has been found in the Mariposa Grove with six thousand rings in it. If such is the case, though I rather doubt it, can this tree be six thousand years old?' At this point Mr. Marshall refers to the remarks just quoted by Sir Joseph Hooker. We can personally vouch for the accuracy of Mr. Marshall's statement as to the tree he and his friend examined, for he is a 'note-taker' of unusual excellence; and the slight doubt he expresses as to the two thousand rings representing two thousand years, can be at once disposed of; so that we have evidence, from very recent observation, of the Wellingtonia living to the age of two thousand years. There is a little more of deduction in the statements of Mr. Muir, and it is only the natural wonder that the mere affirmation occasions that prevents us from realizing fully the possibility of an apparently incredible period of tree-life.

VI.

OTHING in the history of the vegetable world is more interesting than the records of buried trees, whose limbs have been turned into coal or stone, preserving, however, with singular clearness, in trunk, branches, leaves, flowers, and fruit, the form and markings which distinguished them when growing under the conditions that were, with more or less of suddenness, changed by some convulsion of Nature. With the forms retained in the coal measures with such distinctness as to enable the scientist to read the history of the past, most readers are familiar.

The published evidences are less numerous of petrified forests—and curious and wonderful indeed is the process by which wood is changed to stone without losing the markings which distinguished it when the slow process of petrifaction, ages ago, commenced. How great and powerful have sometimes been the convulsions which in past times have overturned parts of the world, and changed all the then existing conditions of the life of the plants and animals overwhelmed, can be learnt from the great depths under the present surface strata at which forestal remains are often discovered. Trees are frequently dug out from positions two or three hundred feet below the surface, and the deep waters of lakes often overlie whole forests, although sometimes the buried relics are only just below the surface soil. Occasionally, indeed, the forestal remains lie along the surface of the ground, or are but barely covered by earth or sand—the earth or sand of the new soil which has taken the place of that buried.

Whilst great convulsions of Nature have probably occasioned the changes which have caused forests and individual trees to be buried at considerable distances under the surface, it is the slow movements of land and water that have given rise to the burying of them in shallows of land, if that expression may be used. By the slow subsidence of land, dry ground would be turned into marsh, and the conditions under which its flora had existed being wholly changed, the trees and other plants that had grown on the dryer soil would perish. As the subsidence continued, the marsh would become deep bog, and a new order of vegetation would spring up, but vegetation of a small size—small enough, indeed, to float on the bog's surface. Slowly, but surely, the undermined trees, already destroyed by their uncongenial soil and circumstances, would sink in the depths of the soft mud of the morass. Lower and lower they would sink, until the topmost branches had disappeared. But oftentimes the process of disappearance is hastened by the fall of the tree, when the abnormal moistening of the soil about its roots had caused them to loosen their hold. Falling thus horizontally into the bog, the tree would speedily be covered by its substance, and the final process hastened.

Much the same change would be wrought by the sea, the ever restless and never constant sea, which is continually encroaching in some places and retiring from others. Forest remains discovered buried under existing sands by the seashore prove that where the waves now roll in upon the land, trees once flourished in magnificence and beauty. Immersion for long years—centuries—in water produces the curiously hard and perfect material called bog timber. Immersion in sand or earth causes the marvellous and wonderful change called petrifaction, by which—though the material is changed to stone, and sparkles with stony brilliance—the original grain, and the spots or other markings of the wood are preserved with singular fidelity. By the wonderful and half-mysterious process of Nature which geologists call metamorphosis, this change is effected; earths are changed into rocks, rocks into other rocks, and wood into stone.

Many of these strangely interesting phenomena have come to light by excursions into the body of the earth; but it will be sufficient to mention two. A petrified Pine forest was discovered in

1883 under Lake Tahoe. For many years an appearance as of a bank of moss had been noted under the waters of the lake; but on the moss and some accompanying slimy matter disappearing, it was seen that they had hidden the limbs and twigs, which could, then, clearly be discerned, of a petrified Pine forest. Fifty feet below the surface of the lake lay this wonderful example of petrifaction, and by the use of grappling-irons lowered into the lake broken pieces of petrified wood were disengaged and brought to the surface. Two acres of ground, it was computed, were covered by this forestal remnant. For the other instance we shall quote from an interesting book already referred to, Mr. W. G. Marshall's 'Through America.' 'We drove,' says Mr. Marshall, at page 319 of his first edition, 'to within a mile of Calistoga, and then diverged to the right, leaving the main-road and the corn-fields that bordered it, and ascending through forests the spur of a mountain till, in five miles, we came to the wonderful geological curiosity which I will now attempt to describe. Within an area of about thirty acres, mostly on sloping ground, were lying prostrate and plainly visible, one hundred or more petrified trunks and stumps of trees, the majority, if not the whole of them, lying in one direction; and besides these there were many more (all of them also petrified) which, covering a large area had been simply outlined or partially excavated from the earth and volcanic matter in which they had become imbedded—for as yet they had only been traced, the work of excavation not having proceeded far' (this was in 1879). 'Judging by the dimensions of some of the more exposed trunks, these trees must, indeed, have been veritable monsters. One of them, which has been appropriately designated "the Pride of the Forest," measured eleven feet across the stump, and thirty feet up the trunk the diameter was seven feet. The tree reveals its own growth, for by the grain of the wood its age has been traced to 1100 years—that is, of course, its age before it became thrown and turned into stone. This great fellow lay thoroughly exposed, and, apart from its size, was a geological curiosity in the fact of its having an almost perfect petrified bark ; and a portion of its wood was not only

s

petrified, but was just in its original state, as if the tree were alive. The ground around the trunk glistened with deposits of crystalline silica; and chips of petrified charcoal, so crisp as to break in pieces with the slightest amount of pressure, were lying scattered about, showing that heat had in some way been brought to bear upon the wood before petrifaction set in. Some terrible convulsion of Nature, possibly a volcanic eruption, must suddenly have overturned these once monarchs of the forest, and have buried them out of sight; and as there is an extinct volcano in the vicinity, namely Mount St. Helena (which rises to a height of 3700 feet above the sea-level), it does not seem improbable that such was the case, and that Mount St. Helena had something to do with it. Though this splendid forest of petrified trees had, when we visited the collection, only been excavated and outlined to the extent of thirty acres, it is probable that it extends over a much larger area, as fresh specimens were then being continually unearthed. Many of those which had been simply outlined lay covered with gravel and brushwood, about three feet or so in depth. All the trees, as I have already mentioned, were prostrate and lying in one direction—from north to south. The forest was, I believe, discovered in 1867. To the credit of one "Charlie" Evans, a Swede, is due its excavation and disclosure, though whether he was the actual discoverer of it, I am unable to say. However, he became an early possessor of tho forest by obtaining a grant of the land from Government—before it was known that there were any petrified trees underground; and now he is complete master of the situation. . . . In his cabin he had many fine polished pieces of petrified roots of the trees, as well as some splendid agatized specimens,—all obtained from this forest.'

It is easy to note the *results* of *metamorphosis* as indicated by the changed form assumed by the same chemical substances after the lapse of time, and it is comparatively easy to ascertain that the beautiful principle of crystallization is the agent employed in many of the changes; but who can understand the mystery which enshrouds the ' motive force ' in all these marvellous processes ?

VII

TREE-FOOD.

ROWTH in Nature cannot be effected without food of some kind, and nourishment is as essential to plants as to all other organic things. Here, however, growth will be only incidentally referred to, as, for plants, it is a subject that only in a slight degree appertains to Winter; but the interesting question of food, and the provision that Nature makes for it, is quite appropriate to the season which forms the theme of this volume.

Perhaps to the careless observer who wanders into wintry woodlands, the least attractive object is furnished by the dead leaves over which he

walks. To the artist, the withered leafy floor of
the forest affords, by its strong and varied *colour*,
some of the finest of his effects; and for the reflec-
tive mind there is much of interest to be learnt
from a subject that might appear to have no
element of interest in it.

The functions of plants, as exhibited in the production of leaves, flowers, and fruit—beautiful as
are their manifestations, and quietly and noiselessly as the processes are conducted—are very
exhaustive both of vital force and of substance.
From the soil and from the air, but mainly from
the soil, all the elements that minister to the production of the beautiful fabrics formed by the
mysterious processes of growth and development
are derived. The needful assimilation and *meta-
morphism*—for this last-mentioned expression
may fitly be applied to the elaborating functions
of plants—though the elements which are essential to them are derived from outside, also involve
more or less of exhaustion, and unless with this
exhaustion there were replenishment, the plant
would languish and die. Hence it is that the
vital substances which are withdrawn, must be

replaced, and it is in this direction that the wise economy of Nature is exercised, and provision is made for returning to the plant just those particular elements needed to supply its particular or individual requirements.

How admirably this purpose is fulfilled, will be suggested by a visit to the untouched 'floor' of a forest. There lie, thickly scattered, dead and dry, the hosts of leaves; the dead and withered blossoms, and the ungathered and shrivelled fruit, shorn indeed of the gloss and beauty of summer, shorn even of the exquisite tints of autumn, but rich still in all those essential constituents which make up the glory and beauty of the seasons of warmth and genial sunshine. Except their moisture, which is mostly gone with those gases which compose it, the dead leaves embody nearly all the plant-food which the living ones contained : carbonic acid, lime, magnesia, phosphoric acid, potash, silicic acid, soda, and sulphuric acid, with sometimes metallic oxides of aluminium, copper, or iron, and it may be bromine, fluorine, and iodine, and sometimes salts. The evaporated moisture is soon returned in the plentiful rain of the Winter season, or in the thawing of rime and snow. Then begins a rapid process of decay, and the re-solution of the dry organic constituents of the leaves into liquid, by the dilution of rain. Slowly but surely the process goes on—leaves are turned into leaf-mould, and the liquified leaf-mould enriches, all around the roots, the earth which had, in the previous season, been drained of its resources, to supply the urgent and pressing wants of the growing tree.

The rains of Winter, too, as well as those of spring and summer, and the melted snow, carry into the earth the gases which they had, in their descent to the ground, absorbed from the air, and thus they assist in the process of enrichment. The store of food goes on accumulating. The lowest portion of the surface-soil, where the leaf-mould is perfectly formed, enters at once, by the action of rain, into the soil below; the stratum of leaves, next above, is only half-decayed; and the surface-bed consists of those last fallen, awaiting their turn for decay and final incorporation into the forest soil.

So the process goes on, with marvellous and beautiful regularity, and with wonderful adaptation to the multifarious necessities of the vegetable world. The exquisitely varied loveliness of the forest is due to the marvellous diversity of the processes of Nature. The differences of stem and bough and twig, of leaf and flower and seed—differences of size, colour, form, and taste—are due to the infinitely varying proportions in which elemental substances are combined in the perfect mechanism of stem, leaf, flower, and fruit. And how simple, yet beautiful, is the arrangement by which these differences are maintained! The fallen leaves of the wintry Oak contain just the elements which produced its individuality; and close at hand therefore, when these elements are carried into the soil by the agency of water, are the constituents of the glory and splendour of the succeeding season. So it is throughout the forest, Nature everywhere maintaining the balance, and promoting and continuing the harmony of that variety, which is the greatest charm of the vegetable world.

VIII.

BUDS, BARK, AND PITH.

EYOND — far beyond the highest possible attainments of human skill is the wonderful provision by which the curious and elaborate mechanism of stem, leaf, flower, and fruit is compressed into the tiniest of possible spaces in the form of a bud. No more extraordinary instance could be afforded of the almost miraculous arrangement that can be effected within a tiny envelope than that of the Horse Chestnut bud, no larger than a pea, once dissected in mid-Winter by a German naturalist. Within the minute space indicated were seventeen overlapping and protecting scales—bud-scales are rudimentary and imperfectly formed leaves; under these an incipient stem and four leaves, flower-spikes with sixty-eight separate flowers, within the flowers incipient stamens, and on these pollen. Not always indeed is so intricate a system of leaves and flowers discernible within the dark-coloured envelope of a Winter bud; but there is always in every bud an elaborate and beautiful arrangement for the continuation of the plant. The bud, in fact, is the infinitesimal model of the mature plant, and from it will issue and be repeated, all that has gone before. Buds may be said to be of three kinds; those which reproduce leaves only, those which reproduce only flowers, and those which reproduce stems, leaves, and flowers.

In climates where Winters are not severe, the outer scales of buds are, in reality, leaves. But when great protection from frost is requisite, organs that would, under other circumstances, become leaves, degenerate into mere scales, which fall off and wither when the real leaves are unclosed. Such scales are often provided with resinous or gummy substances which are water-proof and prevent the rains of Winter from rotting their tender and incipient contents. Some, underneath their waterproof covering, include softest down, which provides warmth and secures protection against wintry cold.

The function of bark is to the stem and branches of a tree what the bud-scales are to the bud. Bark is first a delicate, thin coating of somewhat harder cellular tissue than that which composes the interior of the stem. Inside this is a still more delicate envelope of cellular tissue, called the inner bark. As the outer coating thickens and hardens, the inner one also becomes thicker and more substantial, and both serve as protecting membranes to the sap-wood, the latter serves to protect the heart-wood, and the heart-wood the delicate central column of pith. The larger the surface or superficies, whether of trunk or branch, presented to the cold, the thicker and rougher and warmer becomes the enveloping and protecting bark. It is in its early stage that the pith of a plant needs the fourfold protection afforded by the incipient heart-wood, sap-wood, inner bark, and outer bark. It is then that the function of pith is most vital, for it is the central and principal canal through which the sap flows from the roots to supply all the requirements of the plant. As it grows older, and gets larger, the functions of the pith cease, and the activity of the stream of nourishment which flows through the sap-wood lessens the necessity for the existence of the pith, which then sometimes almost disappears, or, when it remains, dries up and ceases to take any part in the life of the plant. It may, indeed, be assumed that the real office of pith is to nourish the leaves, flowers, and fruit of plants, because pith is always present in an active form in all branches or twigs that bear leaves, flowers, or fruit. As soon as these, by growth and development, have become so large and woody as to cease to bear leaves or flowers, and only give rise to other branches, thereupon their pith commences to dry and lose its utility. In Winter, therefore, there are two forms of pith that are interesting—the big central column, which, if it has not disappeared, has lost its vitality; and the new columns in branch and shoot and spray, not active, but dormant, and waiting the awakening force of spring to force it into active life.

IX

SYLVAN GIANTS.

ERXES figures in history as a great warrior, and not as a lover of trees, ·but that he was an admirer of trees is clear from the related incident of the celebrated Phrygian Plane. The story shall be told in the delightful English of our beloved Gilpin. Says the author of 'Forest Scenery,' taking the account from Elian: 'One of the most celebrated trees on ancient record was an Oriental Plane, which grew in Phrygia. Its dimensions are not handed down to us; but, from the following circumstances, we may suppose them to have been very ample. When Xerxes

set out on his Grecian expedition his route led
him near this noble tree. "Xerxes, it seems, was
a great admirer of trees. Amidst all his devasta-
tions in an enemy's country, it was his particular
order to spare the groves. This wonderful Plane
therefore struck his fancy. He had seen nothing
like it before, and, to the astonishment of all his
officers, orders were despatched to the right and
left of his mighty host to halt three days, during
which time he could not be drawn from the
Phrygian Plane. His pavilion was spread under
it, and he enjoyed the luxury of its delicious shade,
while the Greeks were taking measures to defend
Thermopylæ. The story may not speak much in
favour of the Prince; but it is my business only
to pay honour to the tree.'*

Of another *Platanus* he says: 'In Arcadia, at
the foot of the mountains bounding the Stympha-
lian plains (famous for one of the labours of
Hercules), stood the little town of Caphiæ; and,
just above it, rose a fountain, called the Menelaid
fountain; by the side of which, Pausanias tells us
(Paus. Arcad. c. 23), grew a Plane Tree of extra-

* 'Forest Scenery,' pages 164-5.

ordinary size and beauty, called the Menelaid
Plane. It was generally believed in the country,
he tells us, that Menelaus, coming to Caphiæ to
raise forces for the Trojan war, planted this tree
with his own hands. Pausanias travelled through
Greece in the reign of Antoninus Pius, who
succeeded to the empire, A.D. 151. So that the
age of the tree, when Pausanias saw it, must
have been about a thousand three hundred years.'*
It is said of this tree that, long after, the name
of Menelaus was found engraved on the bark.
He adds : 'I shall next exhibit another Plane
Tree of great celebrity, which flourished in Lycia
during the reigns of the Roman Cæsars. From a
vast stem it divided into several huge boughs,
every one of which had the consequence of a large
tree, and, at a distance, the whole together exhibited the appearance of a grove. Its branches
still flourished, while its trunk decayed. This, in
process of time, mouldered into an immense
cave, at least eighty feet in circumference, around
the sides of which were placed seats of pumice
stone, cushioned softly with moss. This tree was

* 'Forest Scenery,' page 165.

first brought into repute by Licinius Mutianus,
governor of Lycia. Licinius was a curious man,
and not unversed in natural history. Pliny, from
whom we have the account of the tree, has
thought proper to quote him frequently; mentioning particularly his remarks on Egyptian
paper (Lib. xiii. c. 13), and also on that kind
of wood of which the statue of Diana at Ephesus
was made (Lib. xvi. c. 40). With the Lycian
Plane Licinius was exceedingly pleased, and often
enjoyed the company of his friends under its
shade. It was great luxury, he would say, to
dine in its trunk on a sultry summer day; and to
hear a heavy shower of rain descending through
the several stages of its leaves. As a naturalist,
he left it on record that himself and eighteen
other persons dined commodiously around the
benches in the body of it.' *

Going on to speak of another famous Plane, he
continues,—

'Caligula had a tree of the same kind at his
villa near Velitræ. But Caligula's tree appears to
have been more complex than the Lycian Plane.

* 'Forest Scenery,' pages 165-6.

It had not only a hollow cave in its trunk, which was capable of holding fifteen persons at dinner, with a proper suite of the emperor's attendants ; but, if I understand Pliny rightly (Lib. xii. c. 1), it had stories also (probably artificial flooring) in the boughs of the tree. Caligula used to call it *his nest*.' *

These are wonderful examples of giant Planes, and, marvellous as are the recorded dimensions of them, the records are probably reliable. De Candolle mentions, in his ' Physiologie Végétale,' the recital of an Eastern traveller, who reported the existence of an enormous tree in the valley of Bujukdéré, two or three leagues from Constantinople, which had a trunk one hundred and sixty-five feet round ! Its hollow interior was eighty feet round ; its height was one hundred feet, and its shadow, it was averred, covered a space of ground representing five hundred square feet ! In America it grows to large dimensions, and one is mentioned by Michaux—found growing on a little island in the Ohio River—that was forty feet in circumference, measured round at five feet

* 'Forest Scenery,' page 167.

T

from the ground; and another on the banks of the same river, that had a clear trunk of twenty feet, the circumference of which was forty-seven feet. Of yet another enormous Plane Gilpin speaks, mentioned, he says, by a late traveller (Gilpin wrote this a hundred years ago), the author of a book entitled 'Voyage pittoresque de la Grèce.' The Plane in question was seen at the city of Cos. He goes on to say,—

'It stands in the centre of the market-place, and overspreads the whole area of it. But its vast limbs, bending with their own weight, require support : and the inhabitants of Cos have supported them in a still grander style than the Lime at Niestadt is supported. The whole city is overspread with the ruins of antiquity, and some of the' choicest columns of marble and granite, which had formerly adorned temples and porticoes, have been collected and brought to prop the limbs of this vast tree. Though the picturesque eye is not fond of these adventitious supports, and would rather see the boughs bending to the ground under their own weight, yet, if they are proper anywhere, they are proper in such a situation as this, where the tree fills the whole area of a market-place with its extended boughs, and is connected with the houses on every side by the pillars which support them. Some such idea as this very probably gave birth to that beautiful form in Gothic architecture of a circular room, whose dome is supported by a single column rising from the centre and ramifying over the roof. We have two or three such appendages of cathedrals in England, under the name of chapter-houses. The most beautiful 1 know is at Salisbury, which I scruple not to call one of the most pleasing ideas in architecture. The Plane at Cos is greatly revered by all the inhabitants of the city. Much of their public business is transacted in the market-place. There, too, they hold their little social meetings, and we may easily conceive the luxury, in such a climate, of a grand, leafy canopy to screen them from the fervour of the sun. To add to the beauty and convenience of this very delicious scene, a fountain of limpid water bubbles up near the roots of the tree.' *

* 'Forest Scenery,' pages 179-80.

Of enormous Elms, Gilpin gives one instance. He says,—'There is not, perhaps in all this country such an Elm as was in the year 1674 cut down in the park of Sir Walter Bagot, in Stafford-shire. The particulars recorded in the family are that two men were five days in felling it; it measured forty yards to the top in length; the stool was fifteen yards two feet in circumference; fourteen loads were broken in the fall; forty-eight loads were contained in the top; there were made out of it eighty pair of naves for wheels, and 8660 feet of boards and planks. It cost, at a time when labour was much lower rated than it is now' (Gilpin was writing this in 1781), '10*l*. 17*s*. for sawing. The whole substance was computed to weigh ninety-seven tons.' *

Evelyn, speaking of famous trees, said,—'To go no further than the parish of Ebbsham in Surrey, belonging to my brother, Richard Evelin, Esquire, there are Elms now standing in good numbers, which will bear almost three foot square for more than forty foot in height. Mine own hands measured a table, more than once, of about

* 'Forest Scenery,' pages 159-60.

five feet in breadth, nine and a half in length, and six inches thick, all entire and clear. This, cut out of a tree felled by my father's order, was made a pastry board.' In Baron Dillon's 'Travels' occurs a statement that ' English Elms planted at Aranjuez, in Spain, by Charles V., and said to have been brought from England, were '—this was about ninety years ago—' about six feet in diameter without any appearance of decay.'

Another Elm is referred to by Gilpin as follows :—' In the wars between Henry II., King of England, and Philip of France, the two kings had a conference in the year 1188, near Gisors, under an Elm which, we are told, covered several acres of land. (See Smollet's " Hist. of England," vol. ii. p. 210.) The truth, I suppose, is that it was an immense tree. Under its canopy so numerous a train of the prelates and nobility of both nations, who attended the two kings, were assembled, that perhaps no tree ever before sheltered so magnificent a company. Some time afterwards, hostilities again commencing between these princes, Philip ordered the Elm to be cut down. As it appeared to be, in no shape, an object to him, people were apt to say, he did it in a fit of spiteful revenge against Henry, who often, when his army lay encamped in those parts, took a pleasure in sitting under its shade.'*

Sir Thomas Dick Lauder published in 1834 a number of interesting facts concerning great Elms, collected from various sources. One referred to a large Elm at Mongewell in Oxfordshire, which was seventy-nine feet high, fourteen feet in girth three feet from the ground, and sixty-five feet in the extent of its boughs. It contained 256 feet of solid timber. A Wych-Elm at Tutbury is also referred to. It had a trunk twelve feet long, and, at the height of five feet from the ground, it measured sixteen feet nine inches in girth. Another Scotch or Wych-Elm (*Ulmus montana*), a tree differing essentially from the common English Elm (*Ulmus campestris*), was eighteen feet nine inches at one foot above the roots, and fourteen feet six inches at three feet. This tree was at Hermandston in Haddingtonshire. Another—mentioned and figured by Mr. Strutt in his 'Sylva Britannica'—the Chipstead Elm,

* 'Forest Scenery,' pages 181-2.

was sixty feet high, twenty feet in girth at the root, and fifteen feet eight inches in girth at three and a half feet above the ground. Its trunk was richly mantled with Ivy. In 1767 there was a Wych-Elm by Stratton Church, which measured at four feet above the ground twenty-nine feet six inches. This tree was hollow. Another, by Bradley Church, in Suffolk, was twenty-five feet five and a half inches in girth at five feet above the roots. A Scotch Elm in the parish of Roxburgh in Teviot-dale, called the Trysting Tree, was, when measured in 1796, found to be thirty feet in girth! The ruins of this tree were still existing when Sir T. D. Lauder wrote in 1834. An Elm at Checquers, in Buckinghamshire, described and figured by Mr. Strutt, was said to have been planted by King Stephen. In 1834, merely a hollow shell, its stem measured thirty-one feet in circumference; yet from it forked two large limbs that subdivided into a number of branches bearing 'a large head of foliage.' Dr. Plot also gave an account of a Wych-Elm in Staffordshire, which was fifty-one feet in girth at the butt end; and the famous Crawley Elm (also figured and described by Mr.

Strutt), close by the road from London to Brighton, measured sixty-one feet in circumference at the ground, and the cavity within, at two feet up, measured thirty-five feet in girth.

Of trees at present growing in Scotland, Mr. Thomas Hunter, the able editor of the *Perthshire Constitutional and Journal*, gives some most interesting accounts in his recently published volume on the 'Woods, Forests, and Estates of Perthshire.' We shall have occasion to refer to several of Mr. Hunter's facts, and in reference to Elms, he gives the following particulars :—An Elm at Moncreiffe girths twenty feet six inches at one foot, and fourteen feet eight inches at five feet from the ground. One at Kilgraston girths twenty-one feet at one foot, and twelve feet seven inches at five feet from the ground. Two Elms at Monteith girth also twenty-one feet at a foot from the ground. But the two finest Elms recorded by Mr. Hunter are one at St. Martins, girthing at a foot from the ground twenty-two feet, and fourteen feet at five feet up, 'with fifteen feet of a bole and a magnificent top,' and another at Carse of Gowrie. Of this last-mentioned tree he says : ' It is about 200 years old, and has a height of seventy feet, and contains about 460 cubic feet of timber. The girth at one foot from the ground, exclusive of all excrescences, is twenty-three feet, and the girth at the narrowest part of the bole, about seven feet from the ground, is seventeen feet. At about nine feet from the ground, the tree breaks into two great limbs, the larger of which girths thirteen feet, the other being very nearly the same size. The spread of branches is about 100 feet.' Mr. Hunter adds : ' The soil here is black loam, with a sub-soil of sandy loam. The exposure is southerly, and the tree is sheltered from other quarters by rising ground and adjacent trees. It is altogether a splendid Elm, and is so much prized that 50*l.* was offered for it about forty years ago.'

Of giant Larches, Gilpin gives us some account, reference to which will be interesting, in order to compare with accounts of present-day Larches. He says,—' When Tiberius built his naumachia, and had occasion for large beams in several parts of his work, he endeavoured to collect them from the various forests of the empire. Among other massy pieces of timber which were brought to Rome on this occasion, the trunk of a Larch was of so prodigious a size, that the emperor, instead of using it in his works, ordered it to be laid up as a curiosity. It measured a hundred and twenty feet in length, carrying a diameter of two feet to the very end (Pliny, Nat. Hist. l. xvi. c. 40). When this Larch was alive, with all the furniture of its vast top and gigantic limbs in proportion to such a trunk, it must have been an astonishing tree. The largest tree that ever was known to be brought into Britain formed the mainmast of the *Royal Sovereign*, in Queen Anne's time. It was ninety feet long, and thirty-five inches in diameter (" Sylva," p. 228). Mr. Evelin, from whom we have this account, mentions in the same place a still larger tree, which formed the keel of the *Crown*, a French ship of the last century. It was a hundred and twenty feet long, which is the length of Tiberius's Larch, though it had not probably the circumference of that tree. The masts of our ships of war, at present,' adds Gilpin, ' are never made of single trees. It is the method to lay two or three trees together, and fitting them close to each other, to bind them tight at proper distances with pitched ropes and collars of iron. But a very noble Fir was lately brought into England, which was not spliced in the common mode, but was converted, in its full dimensions, into the bowsprit of the *Britannia*, a new ship of one hundred and ten guns, in which capacity, I have heard, it serves at present. This Fir was ninety-six feet in length, and had, I believe, the full diameter of Tiberius's Larch.' *

Sir T. D. Lauder's account of certain Larches is interesting. One at Prestonhall, at a foot from the ground, measured thirteen feet three inches; at three feet from the ground, ten feet three inches. Another at Alderston, near Haddington, was fourteen feet eight inches at one foot from the ground, and ten feet six inches at four feet from the ground. Yet another, at Dawick, planted in 1725, measured in 1834, immediately under the spread of the limbs, fifteen feet; at four feet from the ground, thirteen feet; and just above the roots, nineteen feet.

* 'Forest Scenery,' pages 168-70.

Of the Larches now growing, recorded by Mr. Hunter, one at Athole measures at the base twenty-seven feet; at one foot from the ground, twenty-two feet seven inches; and at three feet, eighteen feet nine inches. This tree was planted in 1738. At Freeland is one ninety-two feet high, with a bole of twenty-four feet. At Kippendavie a larch planted in 1738 girths eighteen feet at one foot from the ground, and is eighty feet high. Another, girthing sixteen feet three inches at one foot from the ground, is 115 feet high. A height of 120 feet is reached by a Larch at Dunalastan, though its girth at one foot from the ground is only ten feet three inches. Of one at Monzie Castle Mr. Hunter says that it 'girths twenty-six and a half feet at the surface of the ground, at three feet the girth is eighteen feet, and at five feet the girth is sixteen feet three inches. The height is fully a hundred feet, and the tree contains 380 cubic feet of timber.'

'Maundrel tells us when he travelled in the East,' remarks Gilpin, 'a few of the old Cedars of Lebanon were still left. He found them among the snow, near the highest part of the mountain. "I measured one of the largest of them," says he, "and found it twelve yards six inches in girth, and yet sound, and thirty-seven yards in the spread of its boughs. At about five or six yards from the ground it divided into five limbs, each of which was a massy tree." A later traveller, Van Egmont, who visited the scenes of Mount Lebanon, seems also to speak of the same trees which Maundrel mentions. He observed them, he says, to be of very different ages. The old standards had low stems, growing like fruit-trees, whereas the younger made a much more stately appearance, not a little resembling Pines. Of the ancient trees he saw only eleven; those of younger growth far exceeded that number. Some of these old Cedars were four or five fathoms in circumference. Under one of them was erected an altar, where the clergy of Tripoli and the neighbouring convent of Massurki sometimes celebrated mass. From this tree spread five limbs, resembling substantial trees, each being about a hundred feet in length, and inserted into the main trunk about fourteen or fifteen feet from the ground. These are noble dimensions, though it is probable that the best of the trees now left upon Mount Lebanon are only the refuse of the ancient race, as we may well suppose the best were occasionally taken first. If Solomon's botanical works had still been preserved, it is probable we should have met with trees of much larger dimensions than those which either Maundrel or Van Egmont measured.'*

Mr. Hunter mentions a Cedar of Lebanon at Strathallan girthing about twenty feet three inches at one foot from the ground, and fifteen feet nine inches at five feet up. At Garse of Gowrie, he says there is one, girthing twenty-seven feet at the ground, sixty feet high, and breaking at three feet from the ground into four limbs, the principal one being fourteen feet six inches in girth, and the others about eight feet.

The 'Chestnut of a hundred horses,' on Mount Etna, has a reputation which is world-wide. Referring to it, Gilpin says : 'One of the noblest trees on record is the Chestnut upon Mount Etna, called the *Castagna de cento cavalli*. It is still alive, but has lost much of its original dignity.

* 'Forest Scenery,' pages 170-1.

Many travellers take notice of it. Brydone was one of the last who saw it. His account is dated about sixteen or seventeen years ago.' (This was written in 1781.) 'It had then the appearance of five distinct trees. The space within them, he was assured, had once been filled with solid timber, when the whole formed only one tree. The possibility of this he could not at first conceive, for the five trees together contained a space of two hundred and four feet in circumference. At length, however, he was convinced, not only by the testimony of the country, and the accurate examination of the Canon Recupero, a learned naturalist in those parts, but by the appearance of the trees themselves, none of which had any bark on the inside. This Chestnut is of such renown, that Brydone tells us he had seen it marked in an old map of Sicily, published a hundred years ago. (See Brydone's Trav. vol. i. p. 117.) Among other authors who mention this tree, Kircher gives us the following account of its condition in his day, which might be about a century before Brydone saw it: " Ostendit mihi viæ dux, unius castaniæ corticem, tantæ magnitudinis, ut intra eam integer pecorum grex, a pastoribus tanquam in· caula commodissima, noctu intercluderetur." (My guide showed me here, what I can call only the shell, or bark of a Chestnut tree, but of such amazing circumference, that one of the shepherds of the country used it as a fold for a large flock of sheep.) From this account, one should imagine that in Kircher's days the five trees were *more united* than when Brydone saw them.' *

A Chestnut at Riccarton, in the county of Edinburgh, is mentioned by Sir T. D. Lauder as extending, in 1834, over an area of seventy-seven feet in diameter, and measuring twenty-seven feet in girth at the ground. The Chestnut in the park of Cobham Hall, figured by Mr. Strutt, was thirty-five feet two inches in circumference at the ground, twenty-nine feet at three feet from the ground, thirty-three feet at twelve feet from the ground, and forty feet at the point where the stem divided. Larger still was the Chestnut at Finhaven, in Forfarshire. In 1744 the attested measurement was, at half a foot above the ground,

* 'Forest Scenery,' pages 175-6.

forty-two feet eight inches. It was then reckoned to be 500 years old. Another, mentioned by Mr. Beevor, at Writtle in Essex, was, at thirty-two feet from the ground, forty-two feet five inches in girth; at five feet it was forty-six feet one inch, and at six feet, forty-nine feet five inches and seven-eighths.

A reference to the famous Tortworth Chestnut must not be omitted amongst this notice of sylvan giants. Gilpin remarked of this tree : ' In the garden at Tortworth, in Gloucestershire, an old family-seat belonging to Lord Ducie, grows a Spanish Chestnut of great age and dimensions. Traditional accounts suppose it to have been a boundary-tree in the time of King John; and I have met with other accounts which place it in the same honourable station in the reign of King Stephen. How much older it may be we know not. Considerably older it probably was, for we rarely make boundary-trees of saplings and off-sets, which are liable to a thousand accidents, and are unable to maintain, with proper dignity, the station delegated to them. This tree is at present in hands which justly value and protect its age.   It was barely included within the garden wall, which bore hard upon it.   Lord Ducie has lately removed the incumbrance, and at the same time applied fresh earth to the roots of the tree, which seems to have enlivened it.   So late as in the year 1788 it produced great quantities of chestnuts, which, though small, were sweet and well-flavoured.   In the great Chestnut cause, mentioned a little above' (at page 86 of ' Forest Scenery '), ' between Barrington and Ducarel, this venerable tree was called upon as an evidence, and gave a very respectable testimony in favour of the Chestnuts.' *   This remarkable tree is still alive, though hollow and much decayed, and in a measurement of it, kindly furnished to us by the Rev. C. Greswell, of Tortworth, in 1879, it was found to be forty-nine feet in girth at three feet from the ground, fifty feet at six feet from the ground, eighty-six feet through from north to south, and eighty-eight feet through from east to west.

One more Chestnut mentioned by Gilpin, and still alive, we must refer to.   Gilpin says,— ' After mentioning this Chestnut, which has

* ' Forest Scenery,' pages 188-9.

been celebrated so much, I cannot forbear mentioning another, which is equally remarkable for having never been celebrated at all, though it is one of the largest trees that perhaps ever existed in England. If it had ever been noticed merely for its bulk, I should have passed it over among other gigantic plants that had nothing else to boast, but as no historian or antiquarian, so far as I have heard, has taken the least notice of it, I thought it right, from this very circumstance, to make up the omission by giving it, at least, what little credit these papers could give. This Chestnut grows at a place called Wimley, near Hitchin Priory, in Hertfordshire. In the year 1789, at five feet above the ground, its girth was somewhat more than fourteen yards. Its trunk was hollow, and in part open. But its vegetation was still vigorous. On one side its vast arms, shooting up in various forms, some upright and others oblique, were decayed and peeled at the extremeties, but issued from luxuriant foliage at their insertion in the trunk. On the other side the foliage was still full, and hid all decay.'* The

* 'Forest Scenery,' page 191.

Rev. Willoughby J. E. Rooke, the vicar of Little
Wymondley—which is the ' Wimley ' referred to
by Gilpin—informed us in 1879 that though the
girth of this tree, which was then only a ruin,
could not easily be taken, yet that the line remained where one could trace the circumference;
that six or seven years before, he had actually
been able to measure the circumference, and then
made it between fourteen and fifteen yards! At
Dupplin, in Perthshire, Mr. Hunter mentions a
Chestnut which girths twenty-three and a half
feet at one foot, and twenty feet at five feet from
the ground.

We must not omit Gilpin's account of famous
Limes. He says,—'At Niestadt, in the Duchy
of Wurtemberg, stood a Lime which was for
many ages so remarkable that the city frequently took its denomination from it, being
often called *Niestadt an der grossen Linden*,
or Niestadt near the Great Lime. Scarce any
person passed near Niestadt without visiting
this tree, and many princes and great men did
honour to it by building obelisks, columns, and
monuments of various kinds around it, engraved

with their arms and names, to which the dates were added, and often some device. Mr. Evelin, who procured copies of several of these monumental inscriptions, tells us there were near two hundred of them. The columns on which they were fixed served also to bear up the vast limbs of the tree, which began, through age, to become unwieldy. Thus this mighty plant stood many years in great state, the ornament of the town, the admiration of the country, and supported, as it were, by the princes of the empire. At length it felt the effects of war. Niestadt was surrounded by an enemy, and the limbs of this venerable tree were mangled in wantonness by the besieging troops. Whether it still exists, I know not; but long after these injuries it stood a noble ruin, discovering, by the foundations of the several monuments which formerly propped its spreading boughs, how far its limits had once extended.' *   Of the Lime of Cleves he says,— 'This, also, was a tree of great magnificence. It grew in an open plain, just at the entrance of the city, and was thought an object worthy to

* 'Forest Scenery,' pages 177-8.

exercise the taste of magistracy. The burgo-master of his day had it surveyed with great accuracy, and trimmed into eight broad pyramidal faces. Each corner was supported by a handsome stone pillar, and in the middle of the tree, among the branches, was cut a noble room, which the vast space contained within easily suffered, without injuring the regularity of any of the eight faces. To crown all, the top was curiously clipped into some kind of head, and adorned artificially; but in what manner, whether with the head of a lion, or a stag, a weather-cock, or a sun-dial, we are not told. It was something, however, in the highest style of Dutch taste. This tree was long the admiration and envy of all the states of Holland, and Mr. Evelin, from whom we have the relation, seems to have thought it a piece of excellent workmanship. " I needed not," says he, " have charged this paragraph with half these trees, but to show how much more the Lime Tree seems disposed to be wrought into these arboreous wonders than other trees of slower growth." ' *

* ' Forest Scenery,' pages 180-1

A Lime at Dopenham in Norfolk, described by Dr. Brown in a letter to Evelyn, measured at six feet from the ground twenty-five and a half feet. The Moor Park Lime, when figured by Mr. Strutt, was twenty-three feet three inches in girth at the ground. Its branches extended 122 feet in diameter, and covered 360 feet in circumference, and it was nearly 100 feet high, and contained by actual measurement 875 feet of saleable timber. The Lime at Cobham Park, Sir T. D. Lauder said, was more than twenty-eight feet in girth at the ground, ninety-one feet high, and contained 536 feet of timber. He added : ' Sir Thomas Brown mentions a Lime tree in the county of Norfolk ninety feet high, and with a trunk forty-eight feet in circumference at a foot and a half from the root.' At Lawers in Scotland, Mr. Hunter mentions a Lime twenty-four feet six inches at one foot from the ground, and eighteen feet four inches at five feet.

Of gigantic Oaks, there is abundant record, and Gilpin gives some interesting passages concerning many of the most famous. We must quote a passage or two. Of the ' Oaks of Chaucer,' he

says that they 'are celebrated, in the annals of
poetry, as the trees under which—

> " The laughing sage
> Caroll'd his moral song."

They grew in the park at Donnington Castle,
near Newbury, where Chaucer spent his latter life
in studious retirement. The largest of these trees
was called the *King's Oak*, and carried an erect
stem of fifty feet before it broke into branches,
and was cut into a beam five feet square. The
next in size was called the *Queen's Oak*, and sur-
vived the calamities of the civil wars in King
Charles's time, though Donnington Castle and
the country around it were so often the scene of
action and desolation. Its branches were very
curious ; they pushed out from the stem in several
uncommon directions, imitating the horns of a
ram rather than the branches of an Oak. When
it was felled, it yielded a beam forty feet long,
without knot or blemish, perfectly straight, four
feet square at the butt end, and near a yard at
the top. The third of these Oaks was called
Chaucer's, of which we have no particulars ; in
general, only, we are told that it was a noble tree,

though inferior to either of the others.' (See Evelyn's 'Sylva,' p. 227.) 'None of them, I should suppose from this account, was a tree of picturesque beauty. A straight stem, of forty or fifty feet, let its head be what it will, can hardly produce a picturesque form. When we admired the Stone Pine, we supposed its stem to take a sweeping line, and to be broken, also, with stumps or decayed branches.' *

Of another he says,—' Close by the gate of the water-walk, at Magdalen College in Oxford, grew an Oak, which perhaps stood there a sapling, when Alfred the Great founded the university. This period only includes a space of 900 years, which is no great age for an Oak. It is a difficult matter, indeed, to ascertain the age of a tree. The age of a castle or abbey is the object of history. Even a common house is recorded by the family that built it. All these objects arrive at maturity in their youth, if I may so speak. But the tree, gradually completing its growth, is not worth recording in the early part of its existence. It is

* ' Forest Scenery,' pages 182-4.

then only a common tree, and, afterwards, when it becomes remarkable for its age, the memory of its youth is forgotten. This tree, however, can almost produce historical evidence for the age it boasts. About five hundred years after the time of Alfred, William of Wainfleet, Dr. Stukely tells us, expressly ordered his college to be founded near the *great Oak*, and an Oak could not well be less than five hundred years of age to merit that title, together with the honour of fixing the site of a college. When the magnificence of Cardinal Wolsey erected that handsome tower, which is so ornamental to the whole building, this tree might probably be in the meridian of its glory, or rather, perhaps, it had attained a green old age. But it must have been manifestly in its decline at that memorable era, when the tyranny of James gave the fellows of Magdalen so noble an opportunity of withstanding bigotry and superstition. It was much injured in Charles II.'s time, when the present walks were laid out. Its roots were disturbed, and, from that period, it declined fast, and became reduced by degrees to little more than a mere trunk. The oldest members of the university can scarce recollect it in better plight. But the faithful records of history have handed down its ancient dimensions. Through a space of sixteen yards, on every side from its trunk, it once flung its boughs, and under its magnificent pavilion could have sheltered, with ease, three thousand men, though in its decayed state it could, for many years, do little more than shelter some luckless individual whom the driving shower had overtaken in his evening walk. In the summer of the year 1788, this magnificent ruin fell to the ground, alarming the college with its rushing sound. It then appeared how precariously it had stood for many years. Its grand tap-root was decayed, and it had hold of the earth only by two or three roots, of which none was more than a couple of inches in diameter. From a part of its ruins a chair has been made for the president of the college, which will long continue its memory.'[*]

This chair is still in existence, and the Rev. Frederick Buller, the president of the college, informed us in 1879 that it was placed in the hall of the president's lodgings, where it could be seen

* 'Forest Scenery,' pages 184-6.

by visitors.   He remarked that 'it is in the Gothic style of architecture, and a fine specimen of the carving of ninety years ago.'

Amongst other Oaks famous for their size must be mentioned the Worksop Oak, which, according to Gilpin, was, in point of grandeur, equalled by few trees. 'It overspread a space of ninety feet from the extremities of its opposite boughs, dimensions which would produce an area capable, in mathematical calculation, of covering a squadron of 235 horse.' It spread its shade over a portion of three counties—Yorkshire, Nottinghamshire, and Derbyshire—and was hence fitly called the 'Shire Oak.' The stem of the Fairlop Oak at a yard from the ground was thirty-six feet in girth, and it divided into eleven vast arms, yet not in the horizontal manner of an Oak, but rather in that of a Beech. It overspread an area of 300 feet in circuit, in which an annual fair used to be held. It was, however, blown down in 1820 during high winds. Damory's Oak, near Blandford, in Dorsetshire, was sixty-eight feet in circumference at the ground, and seventeen feet above the ground it was twelve feet. The famous Wallace Oak at Torwood had a diameter of eleven or twelve feet, and was said to be the largest Oak in Scotland. William Wallace slept in its hollow trunk whilst his army lay in the adjoining woods, but not a vestige of the tree now remains, though Gilpin alludes to it as existing when he wrote in 1781, and ten years before that, its girth was twenty-two feet. Queen Elizabeth's Oak at Heveningham, in Suffolk, is still standing. In Gilpin's time it measured thirty-five feet in girth, and it was hollow in the time of Queen Elizabeth, who used to stand in its hollow trunk and shoot at the passing deer. The Squitchbank Oak, at Bagot's Park, near Lichfield, Staffordshire, was, Sir T. D. Lauder stated, in 1834, forty-three feet in circumference at the roots, and twenty-one feet nine inches five feet up. The whole tree was said to contain 1012 feet of solid timber. The Salcey Forest Oak in Northamptonshire measured forty-six feet ten inches in circumference in 1794. The Bull Oak, in Wedgenock Park, Warwickshire, measured in September, 1783, at one yard from the ground, thirty-four feet, and at one foot, forty feet, according to Sir T. D. Lauder; and the famous Cowthorpe Oak measured, according to the same authority, in 1834, at three feet from the ground, forty-eight feet! It is still standing, but the Rev. Thomas White, of Cowthorpe Rectory, wrote to us, in 1879, that the venerable tree had failed very much since he had been minister at Cowthorpe, a period of thirty-five years. He added: 'A year or two ago a wood-ranger measured its present main branch, and found it contained two and a half tons of wood. It is believed to be 1650 years old!'

Of large specimens of the Ash mentioned by Sir T. D. Lauder, the following examples may be quoted. One at Inch Merin, in Loch Lomond, Dumbartonshire, measured, in 1784, twenty feet eight inches in girth, and another at the same place, twenty-eight feet five inches. Both were hollow, and dead and living timber were curiously mixed. A great Ash at Carnoch, Stirlingshire, seen by Sir T. D. Lauder, was then ninety feet high, 'thirty-one feet in girth at the ground, nineteen feet three inches at five feet from the ground, and twenty-one feet six inches when measured four feet higher up.' It was planted about the year 1596. An Ash at Bonhill, Dumbartonshire, measured, at about four feet from the ground, thirty-four feet one inch; four feet higher it measured twenty-one feet three inches; and at twelve feet, 'immediately under the three great arms into which it divides, twenty-two feet nine inches.' This tree was hollow in its trunk. One of its branches measured ten feet four inches, another eleven feet, and the third twelve feet in girth! We must extract verbatim one passage relating to an Ash from Sir T. D. Lauder: 'An Ash in the churchyard of Kilmalie, in Lochaber, was long considered as the largest and most remarkable tree in the Highlands. It was held in reverence by Lochiel and his numerous kindred and clan for many generations, which probably hastened its destruction, for in the year 1746 it was burnt by the brutal soldiery to the ground. Its remains were examined on the 23rd of October, 1764. Its circuit at the ground could then be traced, most parts of the circumference of the putrid trunk being several inches, and others about a foot, above the surface of the earth. Its diameter in one direction was seventeen feet three inches, and the cross diameter twenty-one feet. Its circumference at the ground, taken in presence of Henry Butler, Esq., of Fascally, and Mr. Campbell, collector of the Customs at Fort William, was fifty-eight feet! It stood in a rich, deep soil, only about thirty feet above the level of the sea, in Lochiel, with a small rivulet running within a few paces of it. No information could be obtained as to the exact size of the trunk. A person present, who had been well acquainted with the tree, described it as being of vast bulk, but not tall, as it divided into three great arms at about eight feet above the ground. The place was visited again in 1771, when all vestiges of the tree were obliterated. The circumference of this tree is greater even than that of any Ash that has been yet noticed in any part of Scotland. But if the Bonhill tree could be measured at the ground, it would probably be found to girth as much.'

An Ash 400 years old at the presen time is described by Mr. Hunter. It stands at Ochtertyre, Perthshire, and is thirty-four feet ten inches at one foot from the ground, and twenty feet eight inches at five feet, with a spread of branches of seventy feet. The trunk is slit and hollow, the aperture in the side being only large enough to just insert the arm. Another at Carse of Gowrie girths thirty-two feet at the base, twenty-five feet at one foot from the ground, nineteen feet at three feet from the ground, and seventeen at five feet, the bole being twenty-seven feet long. But these measurements are thrown into the shade by those of an Ash at Logierait, in Perthshire, the girth of which is, at eleven feet from the ground, twenty-two feet; at three feet, forty feet; and at the ground, fifty-three and a half feet! The height of this tree is now sixty feet, but Mr. Hunter says, ' The height is said to have been ninety feet at one time, but the top was blown away. There is an opening of five feet nine inches on the south side, and the trunk is perfectly hollow. Maimed as it is, it has still the enormous girth of forty-seven feet seven inches at one foot from the ground, and thirty-two feet five inches at five feet, so that in its perfect state it must have been a very great tree indeed.

x

. . . . . The main trunk is thickly covered with Ivy.'

From the Ash, let us revert to the Beech. The Knole Park (Kent) Beech, mentioned by Mr. Strutt in his 'Sylva Britannica,' measured, in 1834, twenty-four feet at three feet from the ground, and at ten feet up, it was twenty-seven feet. It rose to a height of 105 feet, and was computed to contain 498 feet of solid timber; and Sir T. D. Lauder speaks of one twenty-six feet six inches at the surface of the ground, and twenty feet at two feet high. Mr. Hunter mentions one at Taymouth, in Perthshire, which girthed, ten years ago, twenty-seven feet at one foot from the ground, the present girth, owing to one of its great limbs being broken off since—the limb having probably forked from near to the ground—being twenty-four feet six inches, and twenty-one feet at five feet up; and another, at Lawers, has a girth of twenty-one feet at one foot from the ground. One of the finest and most beautiful of Beeches in England is the Queen Beech, at Mark Ash, in the New Forest.

Of Sycamores, there are many records of abnormal size. Mr. Strutt figured one which was
at Bishopton, Renfrewshire. It was twenty feet
in girth at the bole. Sir T. D. Lauder mentioned
another at Calder House, in the county of Edinburgh measuring twenty feet three inches at the
ground. It was planted, it was believed, before
the Reformation, and was, it was considered in
1834, not less than 300 years old. A Sycamore
at Newbottle Abbey measured twenty-four feet
four inches at two feet from the ground, and was
seventy feet high. One at Cobham Park measured
twenty-six feet in circumference at the ground,
and was ninety-four feet high ; and the Kippen-
ross Sycamore was, in 1801, twenty-eight feet
nine inches in girth. Of this famous tree Mr.
Hunter says, ' Unfortunately, it is now in ruins,
but sufficient remains to attest its former greatness. The first damage it received was in 1827,
when it was struck by lightning, and it never got
the better of this injury. The late laird has
affixed a brass tablet to the shattered trunk,
bearing the following description of the tree
before it received its fatal blow : ' Cubic contents

in 1821, 875 feet.   In 1841, girth of the smallest part of the trunk, nineteen feet six inches; girth where the branches spread, twenty-seven feet four inches; girth, close to the ground, forty-two feet seven inches; height, 100 feet.   Extreme width of branches, 114 feet. Age, 440 years.' The age was discovered from some old estate papers.   Another large Sycamore, at Castle Menzies, is twenty-three feet eleven inches at one foot from the ground, and at five feet, seventeen feet six inches.   'It is,' says Mr. Hunter, ' eighty feet high, and has a splendid bole of forty feet . . . the spread of branches is eighty-five feet, and it contains upwards of 1000 cubic feet of timber.'   Another Sycamore in the same neighbourhood, at two feet from the ground, girths twenty-eight feet six inches, and at five feet from the ground, nineteen feet three inches.

One of the remnants of ' Great Birnam Wood ' is a Sycamore at Murtle, referred to by Mr. Hunter.   It girths nineteen feet eight inches at five feet from the ground, and is believed to be 1000 years old.   One at Ardoch is twenty-four feet in girth, the girth above the swell being eleven feet.'

Yews also claim a place amongst sylvan giants. Sir T. D. Lauder mentioned, in 1834, the Yew tree at Ankerwyke House, near Staines, supposed to be then 1000 years old, the diameter of which, as given by Mr. Strutt, was twenty-seven feet eight inches at three feet from the ground, and thirty-two feet five inches at eight feet from the ground. ' Above this it throws out five principal limbs, which are respectively, five feet five inches, six feet ten inches, five feet seven inches, five feet seven inches, and five feet nine inches in girth. Above these branches the trunk measures twenty-eight feet eight inches in girth. At twelve feet from the ground branches spring forth in every direction, forming a magnificent umbrageous head forty-nine feet six inches high, and extending 207 feet.' The Dibden Yew, in the New Forest, referred to by Gilpin, was thirty feet in girth above the roots. One at Crowhurst was also thirty feet in girth, whilst one at Braburne Churchyard, Kent, was sixty feet in girth, and Evelyn reported that near Winchester there was

'such another monster.' At Hensor, Buckinghamshire, there was one twenty-seven feet in
diameter, or about eighty-one feet in girth! Of
the Dibden Yew just referred to, Mr. Gascoigne
Roy informed us, in 1879, that it had disappeared,
but that there was close to the spot where the
old tree stood, 'a juvenile Yew, of something over
a hundred years old,' possibly a seedling from the
old one.   But about the same time a correspondent
at Perth, Mr. James Gaudie, informed us that the
famous Fortingall Yew, referred to by Gilpin as
being fifty-six and a half feet in circumference,
was then (in 1879) still in existence. It is supposed to be between 2500 and 2700 years of age!
although it should be mentioned that, according
to a theory expressed by Sir Robert Christison in
a paper on 'The Exact Measurement of Trees,'
read to the Edinburgh Botanical Society in July,
1879—a paper printed in their 'Transactions'—
the age of this Yew would have been 3000 years
in 1768-9, and consequently more than 3100 years
old now! This wonderful tree has given a wide
reputation to the place where it grows, as is
testified by the lines,—

'Famed Fortingall, whose aged Yew
Still braves the tempest's shock.'

The Horse Chestnut has scarcely obtained fame amongst sylvan giants; but one mentioned by Mr. Hunter is qualified to enter the list. He thinks it is the largest in Scotland, if not in Britain. At five feet from the ground it girths nineteen feet, and at a foot from the ground twenty feet six inches!

Giants, however, as, amongst their species, the trees we have enumerated are, they are comparatively insignificant when compared with the enormous Wellingtonias. We shall therefore fitly close this chapter by an interesting and most instructive extract from Mr. W. G. Marshall's most interesting book 'Through America.' The excerpt is from the chapter entitled 'The Giant Trees of Calaveras.' Mr. Marshall says,—

'The Calaveras Grove contains between ninety and a hundred "big" specimens of the *Wellingtonia*, or *Sequoia gigantea*, which spring up in the thick forest comparatively close to each other, all within an area of fifty acres.

Running up as straight as arrows to the height of some of the loftiest buildings in the world, these vegetable monsters are, we shall see, no less remarkable for the prodigious girth of their trunks. There are trees in this grove over 300 feet high, and one prostrate trunk measures more than 400 feet. Let us take the last mentioned. It has been called the " Father of the Forest," and measures 430 feet in length,—that is, it is 102 feet higher than is the top of St. Paul's Cathedral above the ground, or but thirty-eight feet lower than the top of the spire of Strasbourg Minster. This veteran measures 110 feet in circumference at the base, and the trunk runs for 210 feet before the first branch is thrown out. Three hundred feet up the trunk there occurs a break, owing to the tree having come into collision with another as it fell to the ground. The girth of the trunk at this point—300 feet from the roots—is eighteen feet. The trunk is mostly hollow, for there is a tunnel inside extending for 200 feet, and along thirty-five feet of this there is height and room enough to ride about on horseback, right inside the tree.

By means of a ladder an ascent can be made to the top of the fallen trunk, and here one can enjoy a walk before breakfast of a morning, and acquire a good appetite for it by pacing backwards and forwards. Care, however, must be taken to keep on the move all the while, for the bark is so rotten that swarms of earwigs and stinging insects have made themselves a home upon it; so that if you loitered at all, the consequences would be serious. After the " Father " we will take the " Mother of the Forest." The tree so called stands at the far end of the enclosure away from the hotel, and is 327 feet high, being the tallest standing tree in the grove. Not a vestige of foliage is there upon it, for it rears itself a gigantic dead trunk, mostly bare, since the bark has been stripped to a height of 116 feet, and nearly all the remainder has been destroyed by the ravages of fire. The bark so removed was taken to the Crystal Palace, Sydenham, and there set up; but it was unfortunately destroyed by the fire which consumed a portion of that building in December, 1866. This tree, barkless as it is, has a circumference of seventy-eight feet, and it throws out its first branch at a height of 137 feet. A great living wonder is the " Pioneers' Cabin," which stands over 300 feet high, and is so called from a large recess or cavern in the lower part of the trunk, which is capacious enough to comfortably seat a large family party at breakfast. The circumference of this tree five feet above the ground is ninety feet, by our admeasurement. There is a grand prostrate monster, called the " Burnt Tree," which measures 330 feet in length, and has a circumference of ninety-seven feet. It is hollowed from repeated fires, and one can ride on horseback into the trunk for a distance of sixty feet—in one way and out the other. " Keystone State " and " General Jackson " grow respectively to heights of 325 feet and 319 feet, and " Daniel Webster " has a height of 307 feet. Perhaps one of the most striking sights in the grove is the " Three Graces," or " Em, Carrie, and Belle," as they are called. They stand but a few feet apart, and with their branches intermingling run up to an almost equal height of 262 feet, this being the height of the tallest " Grace." The same with the " Mother and her Sons."

Running up to about the same height as the Graces, the trio stand in close proximity to each other, and one of them, the Mother, is fat and bulky,—she is over fifty feet in circumference,—but her children beside her are slim and "lanky." The "Siamese Twins," too, are great curiosities. There are two sets of this particular species of twins in this grove, the specimens in each being a little under 300 feet high, both sets of twins having the peculiarity of union some forty or fifty feet above the ground, which makes them, indeed, very wonderful curiosities. The greatest wonder, however, has yet to be mentioned. This is a big monster which has been purposely thrown, having been severed six feet above the ground and a pavilion built on the remaining stump, which has been converted into a theatre and a ball-room. On this stump, dramatic performances have been held; and the surface having been properly smoothed over, upon it a dance is indulged in occasionally by the guests at the hotel, sixteen couples having danced upon it at one time; and again, the *cotillon* has been performed upon it by twenty couples ! We measured the dancing-space across, and found the exact diameter twenty-eight feet eight inches. This stump has also been utilized as a newspaper office, for upon it, in 1858, the *Big Tree Bulletin* used to be printed. It took five men twenty-two days to cut in twain this monster tree, by boring it through with pump augers, and even then it would not fall, for it required three additional days before it could be induced, by means of bolts driven in at the side, to quit its ancient foundation. This tree is said to have been over 300 feet in height. The girth of the stump is ninety-six feet. Besides those already mentioned, there are other gigantic specimens, all more or less remarkable for their immensity of height as for their hugeness of bulk, and to some the Americans have given the names of their worthiest men, past and present, and have also been good enough to honour our nation by affixing to a few the names of some of our well-known people. Thus there is " John Bright " and " Richard Cobden " standing side by side. " Miss Burdett Coutts " and " Florence Night-ingale " are also fine trees. (The last named was originally called the " Nightingale " simply ; but in 1865 the word "Florence" was added, to perpetuate the memory of Miss Florence Nightingale.) The following is a list of a few other trees we noted : "George Washington;" "Abraham Lincoln;" "Lafayette;" "U. S. Grant;" "W. T. Sherman;" "J. B. McPherson;" "Henry Ward Beecher;" "Columbus;" "Sir John Franklin;" "Humboldt;" "Dr. John Torrey;" "Prof. Asa Grey;" "Longfellow;" "Wm. Cullen Bryant;" "Prof. James Dana;" "Sir Joseph Hooker;" "John Lindley;" "Phil Sheridan;" "Elihu Burritt;" "General Sutter;" "Bishop Kip;" "General Scott;" "Major-Gen. G. A. Thomas;" "Dr. Kane;" "Andrew Jackson;" "Daniel O'Connell;" "Henry Clay;" "Uncle Sam;" "Uncle Tom's Cabin;" "Old Maid;" "Old Bachelor;" "Old Dominion;" "Old Republican," &c.

'Sugar and Pitch Pines, Douglas Spruces and Cedars, spring up thickly in this grove, growing to immense heights; but they seem entirely dwarfed when regarded by the side of the Giant Tree. Throughout the inclosure the ground is bestrewn with cones of an enormous size, some eighteen to twenty inches in length—these being the cones of the Pitch Pine, not those of the *Wellingtonia*, which, curiously enough, are very small, not much larger than a hen's egg.

' The Calaveras Grove lies about 4700 feet above the sea-level. It was first sighted in the year 1850, by Messrs. Wooster and Whitehead; and as it was the first collection of these trees discovered, it may be said that it was in this year that these giant specimens of the taxodium family became known to civilization. Since then six " groves " have been discovered, all lying in the Sierra Nevada. In the Mariposa Grove, already mentioned, there are 365 Giant Trees, and 125 of them have a girth of forty feet. The other groves are the South Park, with 1380 trees; the South Tuolumne, with thirty trees; the San Joaquin, with 700 trees; the Fresno, with 500 trees; and a long belt extending for fifty miles between the King's and Kaweah Rivers, where there are several thousand. The South Park Grove is only five miles from the Calaveras Grove.'

X.

SYLVAN NOMENCLATURE.

ULL of suggestiveness as trees are, it is not surprising that so large a number of towns and villages have adopted the names of the particular species of sylvan growth abounding in their neighbourhoods. At the beginning of settlements in wooded country, emigrants have often regarded trees with enmity. Such has been to a large extent the feeling in America and some other places. The immense and trying labour of clearing the ground has doubtless given rise to this feeling; but with the rapid disappearance of what was at the commencement regarded as a nuisance, the natural love for trees has returned, and in England especially, where trees are loved, as perhaps they are never loved elsewhere, has the tree-love suggested the names of places.

Oftentimes it will be found that the link is lost which connects the particular name of a place with the trees that suggested it. The particular trees may have been cut down long ago and forgotten; but the name survives to perpetuate its sylvan history. There may be no more a wood of Limes at Lyndhurst, there may be no Oaks at Oakville, Elms at Elmley, or Ashes at Ashton; but still the names will always suggest—at least—a probability of sylvan origin.

In giving the names, which will follow, of towns and villages, and even cities with a sylvan ring about them, it is by no means suggested that, in every case, they were originated in connection with trees; and to have investigated every instance given would, it is obvious, have involved nearly the labour of a lifetime. What is stated, is stated suggestively, and with the hope that to those who live in towns with sylvan names, an inquiry is originated which may have for them a deep and peculiar interest.

Here also, as in a previous chapter, an alphabetical arrangement is adopted as a convenience to the reader and student. Names will be given without comment :—

Acton (Oak-town), Almond, Almond Glen, Amand (Saint) — French for Almond — Amherst (Amhurst), Anholt (*holt*, from the Saxon *holt*, and the German *holz*, meaning a wood or woodland), Apple, Appleby, Applecross, Appledore (Appledorée), Applegarth, Applethwaite (a 'thwaite' is, according to Webster, 'a plain parcel of ground, cleared of wood and stumps, enclosed and converted to tillage'), Appleton (Apple-town), Appling, Arbois, Arborfield, Ash, Ashampstead (field or place of Ashes), Ash-Bocking, Ashborne, Ashbourne, Ashbrittle, Ashburnham, Ashburton, Ashbury (Ashborough), Ashby, Ashchurch, Ashcombe, Ashcott, Ashdon ('don,' from the Celtic *dun*, a hill-fort), Ashe, Ashen, Ashenden, Asheville, Ashfield, Ashford, Ashill, Ashingdon ('ing' in Saxon means a meadow or pasture), Ashington, Ashley ('ley' in Anglo-

Saxon is a pasture in a forest), Ashmanhaugh
('haugh'—from Anglo-Saxon *haef*, an enclosure,
or *haga*, a hedge; Danish *hauge*, a garden—
means a low-lying meadow), Ashmansworth,
Ashmore (*mor* in Saxon signified a hill, *moran*, a
root), Ashover, Ashow, Ashperton, Ashprington,
Ash Priors, Ashreigney, Ashtabula, Ashtead (Ashstead), Ashted, Ashton, Ashurst (Ash-hurst, *hurst*
or *hirst*, from the Saxon *hurst* or *hyrst*, meaning a
wood or grove), Ashwater, Ashwell, Ashwelthorpe
(*welthorpe* may possibly be read *wold-thorpe*, from
the Saxon *wald* and *weald*, a wood or plain, and
thorpe—from the Saxon *thorpe*, Danish *dorp* or
torp, and German *dorf*—meaning a dwelling-place,
homestead, or hamlet), Ashwick (*wick*—from the
Latin *vicus*, Saxon *wic* or *wyc*—means a village or
mansion), Ashwicken (*wicken* may be the old plural
of *wick*), Ashworth, Bathurst, Baydon (in some
parts of America, a bay is a tract of land covered
with Bay trees), Bayfield, Bayford, Bayston,
Bayswater, Bayton, Bayril, Beach, Beachampton,
Beachley, Beaconsfield (a place of Beeches, from
bace or *boc*, the Saxon for Beech), Beaminster
(*beam* was the Saxon for a tree, and *minster*,

from the Saxon *minstre* or *mynster*, meant an
outpost of the church; hence Beaminster might
have meant a church amongst trees), Beechworth,
Beamish, Beechy Point, Berry, Birch, Birchanger,
Birchfield, Birchincliffe, Birchington, Bircholt,
(Birch-holt,) Birchover, Bishopswood, Blackrod,
Bloom, Bloomington, Boiscommon, Boisdale,
Bole, Bolnhurst, Bosbury (*Bos* probably comes
from the French *bois*, a wood), Boscombe, Bosham,
Bosherston, Bosley, Bosall, Boston, Bow, Bowden,
Bowdon, Bower, Bowers, Bowthorpe, Box, Box-
ford, Boxgrove, Boxhill, Boxley, Boxmoor, Box-
ted (Box-stead), Boxwell, Boxworth, Bracken,
Brackenfield, Brackley (Brackenley, possibly
meaning a forest-glade covered with Bracken),
Bracon Ash, Braintree, Brampton Ash, Branch,
Branxholm, Braywood, Bredhurst, Brentwood,
Brewood, Briercliffe, Brierfield, Brierley, Bring-
hurst, Broadwood, Brockenhurst (Boarwood),
Bromfield (Broomfield), Bromham, Bromley,
Brompton, Bromsgrove, Bromwich, Bromyard,
Broom, Broome, Broomfield, Broomfleet, Broom-
hall, Broxholme, Budleigh, Budworth, Burcombe,
Burford, Burgate, Burntwood, Burtonwood, Bur-

stead, Burstock, Burston, Bushbury, Bush End, Bushey, Bushey Heath, Bushley, Bussage (perhaps from the French *boisage*, woodwork), Bythorn, Campsey-Ash, Capenhurst, Cawood, Cawthorn, Chalgrove, Charlwood, Charnwood, Cheadle Holme, Chelwood, Cherry Burton, Cherry Hinton, Cherry Wellingham, Chipstead, Chipstable, Chislehurst, Chorley Wood, Cold Ash, Cold Ashley, Cold Ashton, Coldhurst, Collingtree, Collyhurst, Combe Pyne (Pine), Copgrove, Cornwood, Cosgrove, Crab, Crab Orchard, Cranberry, Crowhurst, Dale, Daleville, Deal, Deerhurst, Denholm, Dingle, Dodder, Doddinghurst, Doningtonwood, Eastwood, Eaton-under-Heywood, Eden, Elm, Elmbridge, Elmdon, Elmham, Elmley, Elmly, Elmore, Elmsett, Elmstead, Elmsted, Elmsthorpe, Elmstone, Elmswell, Elmton, Elstree, Esholt, Evenwood, Eversholt, Ewhurst, Fairoak, Far Forest, Farnhurst, Fawkenhurst, Felling, Fern, Ferns, Filgrove, Finsbury-park, Firbank, Firbeck, Firle, Firsby, Fir-tree, Fleetwood, Forest and Frith, Forest-gate, Forest-hill, Forest-row, Forest-side, Frome Selwood, Fulwood, Galleywood, Gayhurst, Gaywood, Glapthorn, Glen, Goodly

Marwood, Goathurst, Goff's Oak, Gondhurst, Goytre (tree), Grafton Underwood, Grasholm, Green, Greenbay, Gravenhurst, Grendon Underwood, Grove, Hackthorn, Halewood, Hamwood, Harewood, Harley Wood, Harpole, Harptree, Harwood, Hascombe (probably from Hazel Combe), Haselbeech, Hatcham Park, Hatfield Broad Oak, Hawarden, Hawerby, Hawkhurst, Hawerly, Hawes, Hawkhurst, Hawley, Hawstead, Hawthorn, Hawton, Haywood, Hazeleigh, Hazelbury, Hazlemere, Hazlewood, Heywood, High Beech, Highurst, Highwood, Holbeech Marsh, Holdenhurst, Hollinwood, Holly-mount, Hollywood, Holme, Holme Bridge, Holm Cultram, Holme Eden, Holme Hale, Holme Lacy, Holm Pierrepoint, Holmesfield, Holmforth, Holmpton, Holmside, Holmwood, Holt, Holtley, Holton, Holywood, Honor Oak, Hopwood, Horton-cum-Woodlands, Hoswood, Hubberholme, Hurst, Hurstbourne, Hurst-green, Hurstmonceaux, Hurstpierpoint, Hutton-in-the-Forest, Intwood, Ivybridge, Ivychurch, Kidsgrove, Killingholme, Kilnhurst, Kingswood, Kirkby Underwood, Kirkhaugh, Knockholt, Knotty Ash, Labyrinth, Ladywood,

Lamberhurst, Landbeach (beech), Lane, Laneast, Laneham, Langthorn, Langton-in-Speldhurst, Langtree, Larch, Leebotwood-cum-Languor, Lee Brockhurst, Limehouse, Limington, Linde, Linden, Lindenau, Lindfield, Ling, Linga, Lingbank, Lingwood, Linkenholt, Linwood, Lockwood, Longhurst, Longwood, Loxwood, Lymington, Lyndhurst, Macclesfield Forest, Madehurst, Maplebeck, Maple Durham, Maplestead, Mapleton, Marchington Woodlands, Marchwood, Mark Beech, Marshwood, Marwood, May, Maybole, Mayfield, Meade, Meadville, Meanwood, Mears Ashby, Melksham Forest, Midhurst, Milton-under-Wychwood, Monkswood, Monyash, Mountain Ash, Much Birch, Needwood, Newberry, Newton Blossomville, Newton Bromswold (Broomswold), Nichol Forest, Northolme, Northolt, Northwood, Norwood, Oakamoor, Oake, Oakengates, Oakenshaw-cum-Woodlands, Oakfield, Oakford, Oakham, Oakhill, Oakingham, Oakington, Oakley, Oakridge, Oaks and Copt Oak, Oaksey, Oakwood, Oakworth, Ochiltree, Orange, Orangeburgh, Oundle-cum-Ashton, Outwood, Owthorne, Packwood, Parke, Parkend, Parkfield, Park-gate, Parkham, Parkstone, Peak Forest, Penhurst, Penshurst, Pertwood Petistree, Pightlesthorne, Pine, Plants, Plumtree, Plymtree, Poplar, Portree, Portswood, Portwood, Potsgrove, Prestwood, Prickwillow, Primrose-hill, Ramsholt Ringwood, Riseholme, Rose, Rose Ash, Rosedale, Rusholme, Salehurst, Saltwood, Sandhurst, Sevenoaks, Shadox-hurst, Shepherd's Bush, Shipton-under-Wych-wood, Sissinghurst, Smallthorne, Smallwood, Southwood, Speldhurst, Spring Grove, Staple-grove, Staplehurst, Steeple Ashton, Stockholt, Stockwood, Stoke Ash, Sutton-in-Ashfield, Sutton-on-the-Forest, Theydon Bois (from the French *bois*, wood, whence we get the word ' bosky '), Thorn, Thornaby, Thornage, Thornborough, Thornbury, Thornby, Thorncombe, Thorndon, Thorne, Thorner, Thornes, Thorney, Thorney Abbey, Thorney Burn, Thorn Falcon, Thornford, Thorn-gumbald, Thornham, Thornhaugh, Thornhill, Thornhill Lees, Thornley, Thornthwaite-cum-Braithwaite, Thornton, Thornton-in-Lonsdale, Thornton-in-the-Moors, Thornton-le-Fen, Thorn-ton-le-Moor, Thornton-le-Street, Thornton Curtis, Thornton Dale, Thornton Heath, Thornton Hough,

Thornton Steward, Thornton Watlas, Threapwood, Tilehurst, Tiptree Heath, Torwood, Treeton, Tuffnell-park, Tylehurst, Tyndall's-park, Upton Pyne, Upwood, Walpole, Warninghurst, Washford Pyne, Waterbeach (Beech), Wavertree, Weston Underwood, Westwood, Wheatenhurst, Whitwood, Wicklewood, Wood, Wood Bestwick, Woodborough, Woodbridge, Woodbury, Woodchester, Woodchurch, Woodcote, Woodcot, Woodcott, Wood Dalling, Wood Ditton, Wood Enderley, Wood Eaton, Woodfields, Woodford (Woodford St. Paul), Woodford Wells, Woodford Halse, Wood Green, Woodhall, Woodham Ferrers, Woodham Mortimer, Woodham Walter, Woodhay, Woodhead, Woodhorn, Woodhouse, Woodhouse St. Mark, Woodhouse Eaves, Woodkirk, Woodland, Woodland St. Katherine, Woodlands, Woodleigh, Woodlesford, Woodman, Woodmancote, Woodmansterne, Woodnesborough, Woodmorton, Wood Plumpton, Woodrising, Woods, Woodselts, Woodsford, Woodside, Woodstock, Woodstone, Woodton, Woodville, Wood Walton, Woody Islands, Wotton Underwood, Wych (High), Yardley Wood.

Although these names are the names of places

in English-speaking countries throughout the world, yet by far the largest number of them are in England. When they occur in other countries it may be fairly assumed that they have had English origin. But whether native or naturalized —or perhaps we should say adopted—the fact of their existence proves a love, to at least some extent, of the subject with which their use is more or less closely connected.

It must be understood that many different cities, towns, and villages bear the same designations so that the preceding list of some 600 sylvan names does not by any means cover the entire number. But it is offered as a tolerably exhaustive list of variations in those names, and with such a promising list of sylvan constituencies the Author trusts he may find some readers interested in what he has had to say of Sylvan Winter.

INDEX.

THE END.

LONDON :
PRINTED BY GILBERT AND RIVINGTON, LIMITED,
ST. JOHN'S SQUARE.